One Starlit Night

Carolyn Jewel

CJEWEL BOOKS

Copyright

Book Cover Design by Seductive Designs
Photo copyright: Woman © Hot Damn Stock
Image copyright © Period Images
Image copyright © depositphotos/Evgeny Karandaev

ISBN: 978-1-937823-50-4

cJewel Books

About One Starlit Night

Ten years away from Doyle's Grange isn't quite long enough for Viscount Northword to forget Portia Temple, or their passionate adolescent affair. Portia, however, is about to marry another man. Northword tells himself it is wrong to interfere in her life at this late hour, but interfere he cannot help, with his words, his body, and the truths of his heart.

Books By Carolyn Jewel

HISTORICAL ROMANCE SERIES

Sinclair Sisters Series

Lord Ruin, Book 1

A Notorious Ruin, Book 2

Reforming the Scoundrels Series

Not Wicked Enough, Book 1

Not Proper Enough, Book 2

Other Historical Romance

Scandal

Indiscreet

The Spare

Stolen Love

Passion's Song

Anthologies

Christmas in Duke Street

Dancing in The Duke's Arms

Christmas In The Duke's Arms

Midnight Scandals

Novellas

A Seduction in Winter

An Unsuitable Duchess

In The Duke's Arms

One Starlit Night

Moonlight A Regency-set short(ish) story

PARANORMAL ROMANCE

My Immortals Series

My Wicked Enemy, Book 1

My Forbidden Desire, RITA finalist, Paranormal Romance, Book 2

My Immortal Assassin, Book 3

My Dangerous Pleasure, Book 4

Free Fall, a novella

My Darkest Passion, Book 5

Dead Drop, Book 6

My Demon Warlord, Book 7

Other Paranormal Romance

Alphas Unleashed, Anthology *Dead Drop*

A Darker Crimson, Book 4 of *Crimson City*

DX, A *Crimson City* Novella

FANTASY ROMANCE

The King's Dragon – A short story

EROTIC ROMANCE

Whispers, Collection No. 1

Chapter One

March 13, 1813. The Rear Lawn of Doyle's Grange, Somerset. Near the Exmoor Hills, England

CRISPIN HOPE, FOURTH Viscount Northword, stood to one side of the lawn and prayed for a miracle. None arrived. He remained unable to summon a blessed word. He twitched with the need to do something besides stand mute. Words, any words, would be better than his damnable silence. Action, any action, would be better than inaction. He managed to force a smile. A minor miracle, then. Hallelujah.

Naturally, a woman was involved in his present difficulties. A particular and specific woman. Was any man's heart ever brought to its metaphorical knees except by a woman? Minor miracle or no, he needed to say or do something to convey how unmoved he was by her.

He tapped the side of his left leg with two fingers. Next, he cleared his throat. Portia sent a questioning look his way. Of course, words failed him. He affected what he hoped appeared to be mild interest in the proceedings; practically nonexistent. He coughed again and dug into his store of conversational inanities. "A fine day."

"Mm." She arched her eyebrows. "A touch cold for me." Her attention returned to the sapling that was the reason he was standing out here in the first place.

He'd known Portia Temple since he was a boy of eight and she a girl of six. Twenty-one years. For the first ten years he'd never thought of her as anything but a friend and companion who by a quirk of fate happened to be female. Pity for her when boys were so superior, and how annoying that she'd disagreed.

For the second ten years he'd managed to set her neatly into a box in which she was devoid of femininity yet continued to exist as his best friend's sister. A woman he avoided, but with whom he kept a friendly correspondence. Friendly. Nothing more.

He did his best not to think about the time between those bookends of decades. Silence reached out and set fire to his nerves. "It's spring," he said. Oh Jesus. Had he really said that? "One ought not be cold in spring."

That got him another careless glance, and he was convinced that she, unlike him, had found a way to forget. But then, in all their years of friendship, he'd always been the one who felt more deeply.

She stared at the sapling, head tilted. "You've been away too long. You've forgotten our weather."

Resentment boiled in him, and he required a monumental amount of sangfroid to let that pass. Forgotten? He bit back a retort but could not quash the sentiment that came with the impulse. He'd not forgotten a damned thing. It was no accident that this was his first visit to Doyle's Grange in ten years. Nor that this was his first time socializing since his wife's passing nearly two years ago. Outside the circle of his most intimate friends and women of a certain reputation, that is. He straightened the lay of his coat and said with sharp intent, "I've not forgotten anything."

"We'll disagree on that." If he'd not been watching her so closely, he might have missed the distress that briefly replaced her pleasant smile. But he had been watching, and he did notice, and it ripped him to shreds.

Jesus. They'd made their peace in letters, and it was all a lie. All those words they'd written to each other were now stripped of that fantasy pax now that he was here. Instead of the two of them moving on in person as they had in letters, they were mired in the past.

She put a hand on one of the slender branches of the sapling. One would think that in ten years she'd have changed more than she had. *He* had. Her brother, Magnus, had. She was remarkably unaltered. Smiling, too tall for a woman, auburn-haired, full of life. It was—almost—as if those second ten years had never been.

While he watched her, she lifted the hem of her muslin skirt and tamped down the last shovelful of dirt around the tree she'd just planted. She was wholly unconscious of his stare. No. He'd not forgotten anything.

Mud coated the bottom and sides of her plain leather half-boots. Spatters of dirt clung to her hem. She'd not been careful when she pinned her hair this morning, for there were curls, and not the fashionable sort. Hers came loose every which way. In daylight, there was no disguising that her hair was more red than brown, and of all things, that was what doomed him. That dark red hair.

To no avail, he reminded himself she was Magnus's younger sister. He had years of correspondence from her. He'd not realized how her spirit had stolen into the pages and words she'd written. Every time he'd read one of her letters, she'd filled a space in his heart he ought to have closed off. He'd not even known it was happening until now. Far too late.

"What do you think, Crispin?" She wore thick gloves of the sort ladies wore when they gardened, and when she swiped a wisp of hair out of her face the careless motion left dirt on her cheek. The breeze sent the curl free to dangle at the side of her face. An undeniably red wisp of hair. Most women with hair that color insisted it was brown. Hers was a deep, dark, secret red. Soft in a man's hands, a river of curling, mysterious color that glinted with stands of gold.

He had been careful, over the last two years, never to make love to a woman with red hair.

"Well? What do you think?"

"About?" His query came late enough that she laughed at him.

"You didn't have to come out here. I told you you'd be bored." She put her hands on her hips. "What do you think about my tree?"

One afternoon, one unforgettable day—God, they'd been so heartbreakingly young—she'd changed him forever, while she went on being Portia. She knew him better than anyone. Still did. For God's sake, she knew him better than the woman he'd married. She hadn't blamed him for his choice. Never a reproach for his decisions, never a hint that she understood he had been avoiding her these last ten years. She knew, of course. She was too intelligent not to know. When it came right down to it, he wasn't blameless either. Not entirely.

"Well." He pretended to study the tree, but he was really looking at her. Her gown was a striped muslin with no bows, no lace, no fancy trim to direct a man's attention to the curve of a breast or the column of a throat. Yet here he stood remembering his hand sliding down smooth skin, the bang of his heart against his ribs because he had never touched a naked woman before, and, Lord, how sinfully luscious she was. Had been. Still was.

He still wanted her. There was nothing so surprising about that. Men lusted after women all the time. But his lust and desire had got mixed up and confused with more powerful emotions.

"It's a tree, not a Venus in marble." She peeked at him, then returned to her study of the tree. "There is no meaning to divine other than God was right to make them like this."

"I like oak trees. An oak is a proper English tree." In London, her serviceable frock would have been thought plain two Seasons ago. This season? The fact was, no woman of his set would be caught dead in such a gown. But Portia had never been farther from Doyle's Grange than the village of Aubry Sock, some twenty miles distant. He was guiltily aware that he'd never invited Magnus *and* Portia to London before or after he was married. The reasons were legion, and not all them were to his credit. He'd wanted to think of her here at Doyle's Grange. Safe. Unchanging. Here in sight of the Exmoor hills where she would always love him with a passion that moved better men to poetry.

"I'm glad you like oaks, but this isn't an oak. It's a rowan."

"What?" He could not stop staring. Before long Portia was going to take offense.

She rubbed at her cheek, frowned, and pulled off one of her gloves. "Have I got dirt on my face?"

"Yes."

She handed her spade to Hob, the man who served as Doyle's Grange's general servant; footman, groundsman, groom, butler, and performer of any other work there might be. Hob stood several feet back, idly tapping the side of his boot against the bucket of water at his feet. The man had looked a weathered forty-five or a well-preserved sixty for as long as he could remember.

The servant came forward to take the spade from Portia. He retreated a respectful distance.

Portia made a few more swipes at her cheek and missed the dirt each time. So like her. Northword knew he ought not stand there like the sexually stunned lump that he was. She'd know something was wrong, and he didn't see how he could possibly tell her that absolutely nothing, and everything, had changed. He wanted nothing more than to take her to bed again, and to do it as a man, not a green boy who didn't know his way around a woman. He took a certain piquant satisfaction from imagining the results of his mastery of that.

Thank God Hob was here because the Lord only knew what he might say or do. He had made his peace with Portia in words, if not in his heart, and as he stood here, seeing her for the first time in ten years, his very soul resonated with all that had never been spoken or put to paper. Better, he thought, if they had done. They ought to have screamed and shouted and accused instead of burying everything beneath a veneer of pleasantness.

"Hold still." He pulled out his spare handkerchief and walked to her. He could, and would, control his base urges. He put one hand underneath her chin, turned her face to the side, and wiped at the dirt. The smudge proved more stubborn than was safe for him. Her lips were full, that bottom lip so tender. Yet another delicate curve. Once, he would he have stolen a kiss. Taken it. Shared it.

"Hurry," she said. "It's cold."

"It isn't."

"It is." She blinked while he worked at the smudge. He remembered the way her eyes had fluttered closed when he had somehow managed to bring her pleasure during their mutual discovery and clumsiness. Too quick the first time. But slow and tender the next. Oh, the enthusiasm and quick recovery of youth during those weeks that he thought, stupidly, they would continue to escape consequences. All that against the deep, wide landscape of loving her.

"What do you think, Hob?" She seemed oblivious to Northword's stare and his memories.

"Well and good, Miss Temple." The man's Exmoor accent was as thick as ever, but, as it happened, Northword had not unlearned how to listen to that accent and make sense of it. "Well and good."

The smudge yielded to him. He held her chin a moment longer than he ought to have. He knew, now, how to conduct an affair—never outside his marriage; he'd kept those vows. "There. As tidy as I can make you."

"Thank you." She pulled off her other glove and shoved it in her pocket with the other one and made an even bigger lump to spoil the line of her gown. They did not have between them the safety imposed by the formality of titles. She'd always been Portia to him, never Miss Temple. He'd always been Crispin to her. It was only the direction of her letters that styled him according to his title.

Crispin. There were nights when he lay awake remembering the sound of his name on her lips as she came to pleasure. His body came alive at those moments.

"Will the lavender be all right there?" She pointed at the plants in question. Again, she was talking to Hob. "Or do you think it will be in too much shade? Too late now, of course."

"It'll be years before the tree's big enough for that." Of course he said *avore* not *before.* Remarkable, really, how easily one slid into understanding that accent. Hob leaned a forearm on the shovel. "Thee and me'll be long gone by then."

With the toe of her boot, she knocked away a clod of dirt. A smile flashed on her face, and Northword thought of the kind of sex that made lovers laugh. "Perhaps one day relations of mine will stand by this tree." She used both arms to describe a tree of immense size.

While she did that, his eye was drawn, inexorably, to her bosom, and he felt an absolute dog for it. She remained lush in her curves, more than a good many women, less than others. They'd be as good together as ever. Better. He knew it down to his marrow, that thrill of animal attraction.

She lowered her arms. "They'll curse whoever planted the tree so close to the lavender."

"Surely," he said from the safety of his London drawl, "they'll wonder what bumblehead planted the lavender so close to the tree."

Portia laughed, and his heart eased, to be followed immediately by guilt at his reaction. Just once, when he and his wife lay beside each other, her hand on his chest in a moment of perilous intimacy, she'd asked him whether he had ever loved someone else. His denial hadn't come quickly enough. She never asked again.

"I hope you're right." She tapped the ground again with her boot. The view of her ankle damn near brought him low. Was he not a better man than this? Well. No. He wasn't. She crossed her arms underneath her bosom, and the flesh above her neckline shifted in the most beguiling manner. "Done, then, Hob? Well planted?"

"Aye." Hob came forward with his bucket and, after a glance at him—was that suspicion in the man's eyes?—slowly poured the contents around the base of the rowan tree destined to be gigantic in a future that would not include him.

"I should like to know what this tree will look like in a hundred years." She eyed the tree, but shot him a sideways look, a smile on her lips. "Don't you?"

He shoved his hands in his pockets. "Strong and tall, I should think."

"Yes. Yes, my rowan tree will be strong and tall."

Quite deliberately, he closed his eyes and imagined a hundred-year-old tree, thick trunk, branches spreading over the house and shading this corner of the garden. In a hundred years, the world would be a vastly different place, and yet there would be this tree, which Portia, the sublimely sexual creature inhabiting his senses, had planted with her own hands in honor of her upcoming marriage. She wanted, she'd told him, to know she'd left something of herself behind at Doyle's Grange. As if she could help doing that.

When he opened his eyes, the first thing he saw was not Portia but an auburn-haired woman with a delicious mouth and a ripe figure. He saw a woman with a lover's mouth and hands. He blinked and forced himself to see her as Portia, his friend. Sister of his friend and a woman he'd allowed no claim to a difference in gender.

In the main, he failed.

Hob backed away from the rowan tree and sent a dark look in his direction. "Don't worry, Miss, if the sapling looks ill for a bit. Root shock, you know." He nodded sagely, but to Northword's eye, his look was tainted with distrust. Hob knew men weren't to be trusted. "Give her time. Don't over water."

"I shan't, then."

"I'll watch over the tree, Miss. Even after thee's away."

"I know you will." She focused on Hob. He, Northword, might as well not be anywhere near. "Thank you. That would be a great comfort."

"Ah," said another woman. They all turned; he, Portia, and Hob. Mrs. Magnus Temple walked toward them.

Portia's brother had married eight months ago. Magnus, it turned out, had met his wife during one of his visits to Northword's London home and had been waiting ever since to have a Church living that would support a wife. As it happened, the living at West Aubry had always been Viscount Northword's to give, which he had done as soon as practical after the previous possessor passed away. Within weeks, Magnus was married. Think of that. Waiting years to marry the woman you loved. Until the time was right and not a moment past then.

Northword had stood up for Magnus at the wedding, which took place by special license at Northword House in London. He'd offered them the chapel here, not even half a mile up the slope at Northword Hill, and been refused. They would be married now, please, not in the time it would take to open up the house. And so it was done. Had been done, without Portia knowing about the marriage until Magnus had written to her. The couple had honeymooned in Bath, where Northword had a house he'd offered to them for a month.

"There you are, Portia." Mrs. Temple arrived at the site of the tree planting and pursed her lips. She pointed at the undisturbed ground between the tree and the lavender. "What are those?"

"It's spring," Portia said. "Crocuses grow here every spring. You cannot hope to obliterate them all."

"I can, and I shall do so." Mrs. Temple gestured at Hob and stepped around the patch of ground where the flowers were opening to the sun. "Dig them up, please." She curtseyed to Northword and went so far as to bow her head. Her pretty blonde head. "My lord."

He bowed. "Mrs. Temple. Good morning to you."

The woman had the most angelic smile he'd ever seen. "Portia, my dear. Might I have a word?"

Chapter Two

IN THE FRONT parlor, Portia stood with her back to the fireplace and smiled at her sister-in-law. Until recently, she'd not needed the ability to feign a smile or good cheer or any other mood. She was learning that most useful skill, though at times she feared the effort would turn her into a completely different person. Alone, she was Portia. Around Eleanor, she was another woman entirely. A false Portia. A Portia without truth.

Eleanor had stopped by the desk where Portia used to sit when she did the household accounts. The household accounts were now Eleanor's domain. Her sister-in-law perched on the edge of the chair and, one hand on her lap, tapped a finger on the blotter. She gazed at Portia with an open, guileless concern that made her heart break.

"Yes?" Portia looked at the chair nearest the desk and decided she didn't dare sit. She wasn't good at interpreting Eleanor's sighs and silences, though it was safe to assume Eleanor would be heartbreakingly disappointed when Portia failed to divine what was expected of her from all the things she did not say.

Her brother's wife was generous and kind and assiduous in managing Magnus's household, and she loved Magnus. She lived for Magnus, and Portia adored Eleanor for loving her brother with such honesty. And yet, other than Magnus, they had nothing in common. Their minds, their interests, did not intersect at any point, and she felt guilty for her failure to genuinely like Eleanor.

The finger tapping continued. "Dear, dear Portia."

She smiled despite her dread of the conversation to come.

"What *are* we to do about you?"

"Nothing." She managed, she hoped, to keep a pleasant expression. Her stomach contracted into a painful lump. "I am content as I am, you know."

"But, Portia, my dear." Eleanor tapped the lump that was Portia's gardening gloves. "You might be brilliant, you know."

She maintained her smile for, alas, Eleanor meant socially brilliant. Brilliant in fashion.

"You've led a sheltered life here at Doyle's Grange. You do not see things as I do." She cocked her head. "If only Magnus had brought you to London. In time, you would have sparkled. I am convinced you would have had a dozen beaus. Some gentlemen prefer a quiet woman such as you are, though I think if you had ever been to London, you would have come out of your shell. I've seen you smile, my dearest sister, and I cannot believe there is not a young gentleman of exemplary manners and family who would not see you smile and fall instantly in love."

"I do not wish to have a dozen beaus or to dance away the night."

"You are not too old to marry well. Imagine the good you would do your brother if you did." She bent toward Portia, so earnest and mistaken. "Our connection to Lord Northword might be of great assistance in that."

"Magnus cannot afford to send me to London so that I may dance with gentlemen who did not suit me. Particularly when I have already found a man who does." She folded her hands together and struggled to match Eleanor's cheerful concern. "I'm sure you did not bring me here to talk of this." She smiled brightly. "Is there something I may assist you with? The household accounts, perhaps?"

Eleanor blinked rapidly, and Portia felt horrible for her relief at diverting the conversation from the subject of suitable husbands. "What good fortune it is to have you for my sister. Without your kindness, I'd have a far more difficult time. Your brother, too, appreciates all that you do here."

"How may I be of help?" She was not safely off the shoal yet. The most innocent remark or expression might send Eleanor's mind reeling off toward ballrooms and dancing.

"If I may be honest—"

"Please."

"It's not so much what you may do, but what you ought not do and say. Especially if we are to engage Lord Northword's assistance."

"Oh?" This, too, was familiar territory.

Her sister-in-law's lips set in a grim line. "I should hate for anyone to take offense when I know you do not mean to offend."

"Indeed?"

"I know you will feel the same when I tell you this. I think that, living here as you have all your life, you are not aware of certain expectations."

"Indeed, I hope not to offend anyone. Have I?" She did not hide her surprise, nor her concern, for if Eleanor, who was made of all that was light and sweet, thought she might have offended anyone, she may well have done so.

Eleanor intertwined her fingers. By now, Portia knew better than to think her distress would last beyond the next twenty minutes, but it was impossible not to feel the cruelty of allowing anything to beset her. Her sister-in-law lived so deeply in her emotions that it was probably for the best they never lasted for long. "You mustn't be so familiar with Lord Northword."

Portia clasped her hands behind her back. "You think I am?"

"You know I adore you and think the world of you." Her puppy eyes softened, and Portia's heart fell at the possibility that Eleanor was about to lose track of their conversation again. "You did wonders before I came here. Looking after Magnus and the house."

"Thank you."

The corner of Eleanor's mouth twitched down. "But, Portia, my dear, Lord Northword is a nobleman. A viscount." She leaned forward. "The head of an illustrious and very old family."

"I am aware." As if she didn't know.

"I thought my heart would stop when I overheard you call him by his Christian name." She patted her chest as if she suffered still. "The proper style, the dignified style, is either *my lord* or *Lord Northword* or, so as not to repeat oneself too often, *sir*. You would know this if you had ever been to London as I have. If your circle of acquaintance included men such as Lord Northword. Men who, I assure you, would not be as tolerant as he. Was there ever a man so forgiving? Besides Magnus." Her mouth firmed. "I think not."

She mentally counted to five. "The mistake is mine, of course. It's just that I've always called him Crispin."

Eleanor gave a frustrated sigh. "But, my dearest. Portia. How can I explain this? All our plans depend upon Lord Northword wishing to do you a service."

"What plans do you mean?"

"He is your brother's patron." She wrung her hands, and even Portia, who wasn't inclined to think much of helpless women, felt that familiar tug on her emotions that made her wonder if Eleanor hadn't hit on precisely the behavior that ensured she would always come away with what she wanted. How could anyone bear to see Eleanor unhappy? "If we are to succeed, you must show him the respect due a man of his rank and influence."

"You're quite right."

Eleanor straightened. "I am so glad you understand. He knows you do not *intend* to insult his dignity. He is a gentleman, after all. A nobleman. But I assure you, he feels it here." She touched the middle of her chest again. "Naturally, he's happy about your engagement, but he's here in support of Magnus as he steps more fully into his position in West Aubry. He'll want to see how the improvements at the church are progressing."

"Yes, Eleanor." It had been a shock when Crispin arrived at the Grange, despite her knowing he was to visit. No longer a married man. A widower. He'd walked in, and her heart had somersaulted in her chest with the same thrill as always. The years fell away to leave her with bare emotion despite knowing that aspect of their acquaintance was over. Over. Over and over. He was a man of the world now. He had been another woman's husband.

"In London, among the Ton, others will misunderstand your familiarity and think you uncouth. Nothing could be further from the truth. For all that you have red hair and make no effort to improve yourself, we *shall* make a success of you. I promise you. Honestly, my dear sister, if only your hair were walnut brown, I am convinced you would have a dozen more admirers."

"I'm pleased with the one I have."

"If you won't do anything about your hair, you really ought to follow my advice as to your wardrobe. When I was in London, everyone wanted to know the name of my modiste. Everyone! Twice I had to intervene when other ladies tried to hire away Bridget."

"Thank you, but I do not wish to go to London." My God. They were back to London and the inadequacies of her dress—yet another familiar topic between them.

"Think what you may do there. *My* family, as you know, is easily as old as Lord Northword's. Why, Ryans have been in Kent since the days of William the Conqueror." Her smile made Portia wish she had the knack of looking so perfectly helpless. "While I love Magnus madly and think there can be no man finer, the fact is Temples are not so old a family as the Ryans."

"We Temples are a youthful lot." She nodded and nursed her faint hope that the conversation might be diverted again. "Not at all impetuous. Why, my grandfather took twenty years to decide whether he ought to move the hen house."

Eleanor frowned and waved a hand. "I ought to have spoken to you before Lord Northword arrived." She fluttered her eyes, and Portia suppressed the urge to comfort her. *There, there, you poor, dear thing.* "I assure you, I did not anticipate your manner with him would be so familiar." A cloud of discontent floated in her cerulean eyes. "If I'd known. . .

"I am Magnus's wife and *I* should never call Lord Northword anything but that, unless it is *my lord* or *sir,* and therefore, you mayn't either. You'll surely meet other men of his rank, and higher, even, and with them you must be scrupulous."

Portia nodded, and it was killing her, it really was, to speak of anything even tangentially to do with Crispin. "I do see. Thank you. You would have warned me. I understand. I'm sure you ought to have."

Eleanor nodded as if Portia had given voice to the obvious. "Everything depends upon your appearance and your connections. Everything." You'd think she was a surgeon discussing treatments for a dread disorder. "You have not my family's standing, but I shall be there at your side to remind everyone. If we have Lord Northword's support, why, you might marry very well indeed."

"Yes, thank you. I believe I am doing so, of course." There were times she was convinced her sister-in-law was clever and possibly even diabolical. Such as now. "But I am not going to London."

"Of course you are. I understand you have an arrangement with Mr. Stewart, but such arrangements come to naught all the time. No woman ought to marry until she has met at least eleven gentlemen who would be suitable husbands."

"Eleven?" How odd. Her sister-in-law's mind often confounded her this way. "Why not thirteen? Or a hundred?"

Her eyes went wide and, oh Lord, they sparkled with joy. Too late, Portia realized the error of expressing curiosity over the number of suitors one ought to have. Eleanor reached for Portia's hand. "Thirteen would be unlucky, and a hundred is far too many. No, eleven is the perfect number. Never fear. I intend to guide and advise you."

Portia summoned a weak smile. Eleanor's fingers were soft and limp and milky white. Which fact brought home the shameful truth that, having removed her gardening gloves, she could see dirt under her fingernails. She drew away her hand and clasped them behind her back.

"I'm so glad we had this chat." Eleanor rose and took a step toward her. "You understand now how vitally important it is for you to be circumspect in everything?"

"Yes, thank you." Frustration threatened to burst from her in one long, terrible scream that dammed up in her throat. A vision of Eleanor in tears kept the impulse under control.

"I'll apologize to Lord Northword for you." The cloying scent of lilies floated between them when she stretched to press Portia's upper arm. "Please, don't feel you need say anything at all. I'll put everything right with Lord Northword, rely on it. I am happy to help you through this difficulty." She threw her arms around Portia and kissed her cheek. "You'll adore London just as I did."

When they parted, Eleanor checked the watch pinned to her bodice. "Goodness, we've hardly time to dress for luncheon. Do wear the pink frock we made for you. That's your best gown. Together we shall dazzle Lord Northword with our beauty."

"Yours perhaps."

She giggled. Good heavens, Eleanor giggled. "Men like pink on a woman."

Portia hated pink. She hated pink beyond anything. She especially hated that shade of pink in that thick satin. The gown was awful on her.

"I cannot wait for London!"

Chapter Three

AT A QUARTER to twelve, Portia walked into the parlor, a silent horror in a pink gown festooned with lace and bows. The very latest in London fashion, she had been assured. In order to accommodate her height, Eleanor had sewn frothy tulle over a five-inch layer of satin stitched to the bottom of the original hem. Though Portia did not entirely object to lace or bows, she objected to their combination almost as much as she objected to the unrelenting pink of. . . everything.

She was early to luncheon on purpose. God forbid she should make an entrance dressed like this. She sat and scooted her chair closer to the table while she exchanged a commiserating glance with Hob. One of Eleanor's early changes at Doyle's Grange had been to put Hob into what amounted to livery when he served their meals. With Crispin here, the costume had been embellished beyond the bronze frock coat, breeches, and heeled shoes with silver buckles. Now his costume included a powdered wig and a tricorn hat that refused to sit straight on his head. She found scant consolation in the knowledge that Hob looked as ridiculous as she did.

Two minutes before noon, Crispin strolled in with Eleanor on his arm and Magnus on his other side. "Portia." He lifted his free hand in greeting, and his gaze swept her up and down. His eyebrows shot up. She wanted to shoot him dead for that taken aback look. "Heavens, don't get up. Please."

He was dressed for the country, but you'd never mistake him for anything but a man of fashion. A man who was not from Exmoor. His toffee-colored hair was too perfectly cut. A grown man now. Not the young man she'd so desperately loved. With all that had happened between them, the awful strain of those last days, he'd moved on in his life. It was she who had been unable to move forward.

Crispin led Eleanor to the table and touched his fingers to the top of her chair while she sat. Magnus brought a chair closer to Eleanor, but before he took his seat he waved his arms in the air as if he were summoning food and refreshments by magical means.

This brought Hob away from guarding the door. He pushed a wheeled cart to Eleanor and then brought over, one plate or dish at a time, a selection of meat, cheeses, cakes, biscuits, and various other comestibles. There was even a pot of coffee. Without a moment's hesitation, Crispin poured himself a cup, adding sugar and milk. So deftly done that one had to imagine he frequently sat down to coffee. It was a luxury here. And a rarity. This, too, was a habit of his of which she had no knowledge. She had herself never acquired a taste for coffee.

Conversation moved from politics to horses to racing phaetons and the state of the poor who lived between Aubry Sock and West Aubry. Portia had little to contribute to the conversation. Every time she looked down or caught a glimpse of the frock Eleanor had so lovingly helped her make, she shuddered.

Hob brought over a plate of sliced duck, and for a time there was no noise but that of silverware against the best china and teacups or coffee cups clicking against porcelain saucers. She stared out the window. Clouds that promised rain all but blocked out the sky. She poked at her duck and set herself to mashing the remains of some cheddar. The thought of eating did not appeal. If this kept up, she'd waste away and become delicate through lack of appetite. She'd never look well in pink, though. Not with her hair. She didn't even want to look at Crispin for fear she'd see in his eyes a reflection of how unsuited she was to gowns with lace and frills. He unnerved her, to be honest.

Magnus gave a great harumph and took a large helping of duck. "Are we ready, do you think, Eleanor, for our journey to the seashore?"

Weeks before Crispin's arrival, Magnus and Eleanor had engaged to spend a fortnight in Brighton. They had rooms reserved at a favorite hotel, and Portia had been looking forward to several blessed days alone. She'd planned to stay up all hours, sleep away the mornings, and spend her afternoons transplanting crocuses to the rear lawns. That, alas, was not to be.

Once they had realized Crispin's visit would overlap with the Brighton trip, Magnus had suggested Portia ask Mr. Stewart to bring his mother to the Grange for a visit so as to avoid any hint of impropriety. This was done and the invitation accepted. As it turned out, however, Crispin had an appointment in West Aubry during the days that Magnus and Eleanor were to be away, discovered too late to even think of putting off the Stewarts' visit.

"Indeed we are." Eleanor put her hand over Magnus's, and there was just no denying that when she looked at her husband she glowed. "After Brighton, London. I hope, Lord Northword, that you will be in Town then, for I know Portia is looking forward to seeing Northword House."

His expression smoothed out. "I don't know my schedule. I daresay it's possible." Crispin glanced at her, but Portia averted her eyes just in time. Having him here was much, much more difficult than she'd imagined. And that hint of distance in his voice? He did not want her in London any more than she wanted to go. The fact that Crispin and Jeremy must inevitably meet only deepened her tension and anxiety. "If I am not in Town or at home, do please call. The housekeeper will give you a tour."

"You'll be in London for the sessions, I imagine," Eleanor said. "I know Mr. Temple would like to attend them while I show Portia the delights of Bond Street and my favorite shops."

Portia did her best imitation of one of Eleanor's helpless smiles. She hated herself for it, but she did it. "I have been thinking," she said for Eleanor's benefit, "that if your London excursion comes off, I'm sure Mr. Stewart and his mother would love to accompany us. Would that not be agreeable?"

Crispin returned a shallow grin. "I should be delighted to show all of you Northword House." He cut a slice of duck. "If I am in Town."

"Portia dearest, are you certain Mrs. Stewart can withstand such a journey? It's such a long way for a frail woman."

Oh, how neatly her trap was sprung. "What a disappointment if she cannot. But let's not despair. I'll settle everything when they are here and write to you at Brighton."

"Have you been to Brighton, Portia?" Crispin pushed his cup forward so that Hob could refill it from the coffee pot. "Thank you."

"No. I've not been."

"You'd like it immensely. Seeing the ocean. Everyone ought to see the ocean at least once." He moved her untouched teacup out of his line of sight.

Candlelight reflected off his hair and turned the darker streaks in his hair to bronze. He was astonishingly confident of himself and at ease with the sort of conversation that took no toll on anyone. "Tell me, ladies, have you bathing costumes?"

Eleanor fluttered her lashes. "I have, my lord. It's new, and I've been keeping it secret from Magnus."

Portia wished she were married already. She wished she were nowhere near Crispin or Doyle's Grange. The light in the room shifted with the gathering clouds, and she seized on that as an excuse to stare out the window. She'd rather count cracks in the plaster than torture herself by watching Crispin bring Eleanor under his spell.

"And you, Portia? Have you a bathing costume?"

"I haven't." She looked away because she couldn't bear that there was so little left of the woman Crispin had once loved. Eleanor made a face at her, and, perhaps a shade too late, Portia understood why. She coughed and patted her upper chest. "Forgive me. My lord. I have no bathing costume, secret or otherwise. But I cannot go to Brighton in any event, sir. And while I should like to see London, sir, I expect that won't be possible. Not until after I am married."

Crispin leaned sideways against his chair. He'd dressed elegantly this afternoon, hadn't he? A far cry from the country clothes he'd worn when he'd lived at Wordless. His coat was the finest wool, his shirt a delicate lawn, and his waistcoat, well, that was heavy silk embroidered with tiny points of gold thread. "What's got into you?"

"I don't know what you mean."

"Nonsense to be so formal, and you know it." He rested his wrist on the edge of the table, and his frown deepened. "I wish you would stop it."

Eleanor gave a gentle sigh. "But, Lord Northword. Good manners are never nonsense. She ought to show you the respect due from a woman of her position. Indeed, to all men of your standing." In tandem, Magnus and Crispin stared at Eleanor. She gazed back with that helpless gaze she'd so perfected. No one said anything for too long.

Crispin took a sip of his coffee. "Portia and I are old friends."

"What will people say when we are in London and she speaks of you with so little respect?" Her mouth trembled. "She will make entirely the wrong impression."

Crispin turned his head to her, and their eyes met. For a moment, it was as if they were lovers still, with none of their mistakes and missteps between them. Her heart stopped beating and did not start again until he looked away. *Thank God.* Thank God he had not acknowledged that moment.

"Eleanor," she said out of pure desperation for a change in subject. "Were you not telling me you have a list of improvements you'd like to make to the Grange? Is there anything I may do to assist with that while you and Magnus are in Brighton?"

Crispin gave every appearance of being as fascinated by Eleanor as he was not by her. Watching him, Portia wondered if his late wife had been anything like Eleanor. She'd never been able to pry much information from Magnus on the subject of Lady Northword, other than to have him say she was the daughter of a duke and quite beautiful. Once, after one of his visits to London, he'd let slip that her health was delicate. Portia had understood that to mean she was in a way of giving Crispin his heir. But there was never any announcement and never any letter of congratulation to write.

"The Grange is perfect just as it is." Magnus helped himself to more cheddar.

"Darling man." Eleanor patted his arm. "That's because you have never known Doyle's Grange to be other than what it is. Of course you love your home. It would be unnatural if you did not."

"Quite right, my dear."

"Change is upsetting, I shall never deny that." She smiled as she cut a slice of duck. From over Eleanor's shoulder, Portia watched raindrops hit the windows, pinpricks of water on the glass. "There are improvements to be made here. Am I not fortunate to have Portia to assist me?" She swept a hand in an arc. "I have such plans for this room."

Underneath the table, Crispin stuck out his leg and stepped on Portia's toes. "What do you think?"

"About what?" That earned her another puppy-eyed gaze from Eleanor. She stabbed her duck with her fork and wished she'd thought to feign illness and stay upstairs in her room. "What do I think about what, my lord?"

"The plans for redecorating, of course."

"Nothing." He was only trying to make conversation, and here she was turning into the sort of dismal drear no one liked at all.

He looked around the table. A diamond winked amid the lace of his neckcloth. The young man she'd known would never have worn a diamond or the fobs hanging from his watch chain. Nor the signet ring gleaming from the index finger of his right hand. "All I know is I've no taste in such things."

"I'm sure that's not so, Lord Northword." Eleanor returned him a brilliant smile. "Why, Northword House is all that is tasteful and elegant."

"My wife managed all that. I was happy to have her do so."

Magnus took Eleanor's hand in his and kissed her knuckles. "Everything I have is yours, as you well know. Do what you will with the place, though I don't see how it could be improved."

"But Magnus!" She went wide-eyed again. "The room is green, and green, my dearest Mr. Temple, is not a color I appreciate."

"No?" He kissed her knuckles again. "Away with it then."

Crispin looked to Portia. His expression was bland, but she was convinced he was taunting her. "What color would you do the room in?"

"Green, I fear." She had been a fortnight with the painters choosing that shade of green and another week before she was satisfied all the colors were exactly perfect for the room. It was six weeks before the room had been painted to her satisfaction. "If I had known Magnus was going to marry, I'd not have had the work done."

Eleanor gave one of her delightful laughs. "One acquires a certain sensibility when one has lived in society. I have seen, as you have not, Portia darling, some of the great houses of London. Northword House, for example. So inspiring, my lord. I am most eager to see it again, and I do hope one day that Portia, too, will see the house so that she will understand precisely what I mean to do here at the Grange. After all, Lady Northword was a woman of exceptional taste, and one will never go wrong studying what she wrought at Northword House." She took a tiny bite of duck. "I shall never forget how kind she was to give me a personal tour when I first called."

This fascinated her. "You met Lady Northword?"

"I like to think we became friends." Eleanor touched the strand of pearls around her throat. "I hope you don't think me presumptuous, Lord Northword, to speak of your wife. I know you mourn her still."

He nodded. "Not at all, Mrs. Temple."

"Your wife and I had a great many interests in common."

"Did you?"

Portia accepted the sting to her heart. She had nothing in common with Lady Northword. What had brought her and Crispin together was not what made a man settle on the woman he would marry. She shredded her duck until she had reduced it to a paste. Half an hour, she told herself. In half an hour, she could plead a headache and retire to her room. Which happened to be green.

"Oh yes, my lord. We spoke at great length of how one ought to decorate and arrange one's home. To be sure, Doyle's Grange can never be on the scale of Northword House, or Northword Hill." Eleanor surveyed the room, eyes moving over the architectural features and, no doubt, totting up all that must be removed, repainted, or destroyed in order to make Doyle's Grange over in the exquisite sensibilities of Lady Northword.

"The parlor, for example, might be made quite lovely. Lady Northword had the most exacting opinions about parlors. She had a particular horror of green, and ever since I have shared that opinion. Even so," Eleanor went on, "there is a charm here that can be brought out. A few of Magnus's best paintings might be hung on the walls, for example." She gazed at Magnus. He gazed back, besotted and beguiled by his wife, and Portia could only feel the hollow certainty that she would never, not in a hundred thousand years, gaze at her husband that way.

Eleanor continued. "Several rooms are in need of the attentions of someone with refined tastes. So as to bring out charms that currently are hidden. Imagine how much more easily this can be accomplished if Portia could see the homes that inspired me. My dear Mr. Temple, we simply *must* bring her to London!"

Portia shot to her feet. Crispin stood, napkin in one hand. Magnus, too, after a moment. "Do sit down, you two." She drew a breath and then found everyone staring at her as if she'd gone mad. Perhaps she had. The walls closed in on her, and she wanted nothing more than to be anywhere in the world but there. "Forgive me. I don't feel well at all."

"Of course, of course." Eleanor stood and pressed the back of her hand to Portia's cheek. "I'll send a tisane to you. You must rest, please."

"Thank you. You are too kind."

She did not go to her room. God, she'd suffocate in there with all that green that was so offensive a color to Lady Northword. Instead, she went out the front.

The heavy door slammed behind her.

Chapter Four

AFTER PORTIA LEFT the parlor, Magnus sat again, but Northword stayed on his feet, in the grip of an understanding that cut to his core. Portia's life and his had diverged beyond hope of any reconciliation beyond the polite exchanges of their letters. It didn't matter that he found her more attractive than ever. It didn't matter that from time to time they fell into the old habits of their past intimacy. The woman he'd loved was gone.

"My lord?"

Mrs. Temple's overly sweet voice grated on his nerves, and he gazed at her, still lost in his thoughts. There was no reason to be concerned for Portia, Northword told himself. She was well looked after here, and before long she would be married and in the care of her husband.

"Lord Northword?"

The so-feminine lilt to the woman's voice snapped him back to the present. Could such naiveté be genuine? The moment the doubt entered his head, he felt guilty. She was a lovely, delicate woman who had never, at any time that he'd observed, said anything to deserve an unkindness from him. But good God, Portia must hate being spoken to as if she cared for nothing but the color of the damned walls.

"Hullo there." Magnus rapped on the table. "Word, you great lump."

"I beg your pardon." He threw his napkin on the table and was in the act of sitting when the front door opened and then closed with more force than necessary. Uneasiness lodged in his gut and expanded to take up the whole of his chest. He did not care for the feeling. Out of the window, from the corner of his eye, he saw a flash of pink and then the unmistakable deep red of

Portia's hair. What the devil was she doing outside when the skies looked ready to break open? She'd catch her death.

While he stared at that flash of receding pink, fat drops of rain hit the glass. She was out there, without a coat or cloak, and quite plainly, and to his mind, understandably upset. She had no one to talk to or rage at. He could not imagine her opening up to Mrs. Temple. Impossible, that.

"Excuse me, please." He forced himself to smile at Mrs. Temple. "I have just recalled a letter I must write immediately. I can't fathom how I could have forgotten to get it into the morning post."

Magnus took a sip of his tea. "Give it to Hob when you're done. He'll get it to Up Aubry for you. There's just time, I think, to make the afternoon post, if you're quick about it."

"Yes, thank you. I'll do that." He bowed and hurried out of the parlor. He hadn't even known his late wife had disliked the color green. Why had he not known that? By the time he'd fetched his greatcoat and hat and was himself outside and heading toward the rear of the house, rain fell steadily. Portia was long past the back gate and moving away from the Grange, her gown a splash of pink against the green of the field.

He started after her. He'd made up perhaps a quarter of the distance between them when, at last, she slowed, though she maintained a brisk pace and kept her head down. When she disappeared over the other side of the slope, he walked faster. Rain came down hard enough to pound on his hat and turn the surface of the path to mud. He lengthened his stride.

At the top of the slope, he caught sight of her again, moving rapidly up the hill that led—eventually—to Wordless. And wasn't that a fine joke that he should call his own home by the name Portia had given it in her letters. Wordless, because he was familiarly called *Word* by certain intimate friends, and he was never at Northword Hill. He'd told Magnus about that, and they'd taken to calling all manner of things Wordless.

He cupped his hands to the sides of his mouth. "Portia!"

Wind whipped away the sound of her name, but she stopped. Then, without turning to look, she darted off, skirts in her hands. Wasn't that just like her, to be contrary and headstrong? He plunged down the hill and slid in the mud, though he managed to keep his feet. Once, she slipped, too, but as he had, she caught herself and kept going.

Water dripped from the brim of his hat onto his face, and wherever the drops hit his cheeks his skin burned with cold. She slowed, and God knows she would have needed inhuman endurance to maintain her pace in these conditions.

He caught up at the stone fence that marked the border between the Grange and his property. From here, the side of Northword Hill rose up, turned a darker gray by the rain.

This time, he did not need to shout. "Portia."

She stopped walking but did not face him. Her hands hung at her sides. Water ran down the back of her neck, making rivers of the tendrils of hair that had escaped her hairpins.

Northword took a step closer. Even if he'd been close enough to touch her, he wasn't sure he'd dare. Never mind their difficulties, never mind the years and the chasm between them, he did not want to see her in distress. Not like this. "Portia."

She whirled on him, eyes ablaze. Rain dripped down her face, and she shivered once. Gooseflesh pimpled her exposed skin. "What could you possibly want from me? There's no need to humiliate me like this. Haven't I done enough to push you away?"

"I didn't come after you to humiliate you."

"Well, you have. Lord Northword." She walked away, keeping to the line of the fence, away from the Grange. The hem of her skirt was muddy for several inches, and the fabric was soaked halfway to her knees.

He followed and raised his voice to be heard over the rain and the distance she was putting between them. "Since when does my chasing after you to make sure you don't catch your death of sleet and rain count as humiliation, I'd like to know?"

The skies opened. Unbelievable as it seemed, it was actually raining harder, and cold enough now that there were tiny pellets of ice. He thought she meant to pretend she hadn't heard him, but then she made a rude gesture. And kept walking. This was the Portia he remembered. Passionate. Always passionate.

"Stop." He took three long steps and caught her arm, pulling her around to face him. Her mouth was rimmed with white, but there was a telltale tremor around her jaws. "We can't stay in this downpour."

"I don't care." Rain plastered that awful pink gown to her body.

"I don't care much if you think I've humiliated you when I haven't."

She stared him down. He did not know this woman. She was not a girl. She'd lived ten years without him, and in ten years people changed. They left behind fancies of love and passion. They married and lived dutiful lives.

"Thank you for telling me how I feel. Now that you are Lord Northword, of course you know all." She pulled away. He didn't let go of her arm, and a good thing, too, because she slipped, and it was only because he steadied her that she didn't fall.

He brought her close and raised his voice to be heard. "It's bloody hailing. We're going to freeze if we stay out here much longer."

"You needn't have come after me." Her chin tipped up in an expression so familiar to him he lost sight of those ten years.

"Yes, I did need."

"You didn't." She tugged on her arm. "Let go."

"You know me better than that."

"I don't think I do."

"You don't at all if you think I'd leave any lady outside in this weather, not one dressed as you are, and not when I know she's upset and unable to think as clearly as she ought."

Her eyes widened, and not in recognition of his good sense. She was magnificently furious. "Let me alone, Crispin Hope, you booby-headed jackass."

He kept his grip on her arm. "Use your intellect, if you haven't let it be worn to a blunt by listening to your sister-in-law prattle on about gowns and London and the proper forms of address. You know as well as I that you'll freeze out here." He pointed toward the dark gray stones of his childhood home. "Wordless is nearer than the Grange. Let's go there and wait out the rain." He brought her closer to him, and he forgot everything that had gone wrong between them, the wrongs they'd done each other. Whatever else had happened, he could not bear to see her unhappy. "You can tell me everything that's made you so miserable. Will you do that much? Please?"

Something of what he was feeling must have transferred to her, for she wiped water out of her face and nodded. "How long have you got?"

"As long as we need. You know that." He ached to touch her, to console her, but didn't dare. She was too angry. And he was too much on edge. "Out of the rain, if you please."

She nodded again.

"Thank you." He didn't give her time to change her mind or form an objection. He swung her into his arms and bodily lifted her over the fence. From the awkward way she reacted, he knew she hadn't expected to find herself in his arms. Nor had he anticipated doing so until it was done.

When she was safely down and steady on her feet, he stepped over the fence himself. He shrugged out of his greatcoat and put it around her shoulders. One did such things for ladies. As an afterthought, he clapped his hat on her head, too.

"Come along, then." He managed a smile that at long last did not feel false. "Before we drown or are killed by hail."

He marched them toward the house and around to the front. He remembered the days when he had run up those twenty front stairs, often with Magnus and Portia in tow. He could see the house as it had been then—the servants, now long moved on to other positions, the interior of the house. How strange to think of those rooms as empty and dark. Rooms where his wife had never been and where she had left no mark.

No great surprise, the front door was locked. The groundskeeper lived in West Aubry and had no need for access to the house. His steward visited but twice a year to see to any interior maintenance that might be required.

Rain beat down while they tried every other entrance and found each door locked and barred, every shutter closed. Short of breaking a window or kicking in a door they weren't getting inside. In the abstract, he was pleased that Wordless was so well protected, but at the moment, he was inconvenienced at being denied entry to his own damned house. Both of them were shivering now, with no sign of the rain letting up and the cold getting sharper.

"The stables?" Portia said.

He nodded and took her hand while they dashed along the gravel drive that led to the stable block only to find the grooms' quarters locked up as tight as the house. They took refuge in the long stone archway of the stables, eight stalls on each side. The block emptied onto a courtyard with the carriage house at the far side. That was locked tight, too, he discovered.

Back in the archway between the two rows of stalls, they stood side by side, dripping water onto the paving stones. He stamped his feet and made a largely futile attempt to brush water off his coat and out of his hair. "At least we're out of the wet."

"Yes." She stared at the rain beating down on the courtyard and cascading from the gutters.

"Tell me why you're so unhappy?"

"I shan't. Not more than you've guessed." She shook her head. He'd give anything to have her look at him. "You'll only think less of me than you do already."

"She rubs my nerves raw, too, sometimes."

"Oh," she breathed. "Awful man."

"True." In the silence he stamped his feet some more and managed to dislodge some of the mud that clung to his boots. "It can't come down like this for much longer."

"Yes, it can."

He'd lived here long enough to know it could rain like this until tomorrow. "Listen to us." He rolled his eyes even though she wasn't looking at him. "Talking about the weather like two old ladies."

She shrugged, but halfway through the motion she shivered. Without thinking, he put his arms around her. She didn't come close.

"Take pity on me," he said. "I'm cold."

After a moment of resistance, she leaned toward him. He eased closer and tightened his arms around her. "Better. Much better." He rubbed his hands up and down her back. She rested her head against his chest, and he slipped his hands underneath his greatcoat and rested them in the small of her back. He wanted to tell her he'd forgiven her, that he'd never forgotten a moment of their time as lovers, but that seemed. . .unwise.

After a moment or two of standing like this, she lifted her head and stared at the waterfall sluicing off the roof. The courtyard's central gutters overflowed. The noise was near deafening. "I don't think it's going to stop."

Like her, he stared at the water. "We can wait a while yet."

"Hob will worry," she said. "Magnus, too. They'll wonder where we've got to."

He continued to stroke her back. "Five minutes. Then we'll go even if it's no better."

With a sigh, she settled against him, tucking her hands between them. Five minutes later, the rain hadn't let up.

He forgot all about the cold and the damp as he brushed away a tendril of dark red hair that had stuck to her cheek. She pushed away, and he did the strangest, most contradictory, selfishly male thing imaginable. He brought her close instead of setting her back. She lifted her chin and gave him a quizzical look. The world dropped away. This was Portia. His Portia, and whatever had happened between them, no matter how they'd changed, nothing had changed at all.

He lowered his head to hers.

Chapter Five

FOR THE SPACE of half a heart-beat, he told himself he wasn't going kiss her. It would be stupid and wrong of him, and it would destroy the safety of the friendship they'd carved out for themselves during their years of letter writing.

His chest was so tight with tension, he could scarcely breathe. He was seventeen again, and his brain was overset with lust and desire and emotions too big to name. His cock was hard with the joy of holding this woman in his arms and at the prospect of being inside her. At long, long last.

Northword didn't move. Didn't breathe. Nor did she. In no way was that fact lost on him.

Her mouth brushed his. Barely there. For an instant, he didn't react. He couldn't. Surely, she had not meant that invitation. She was going to marry someone else, wasn't she? Except she didn't step away, and he didn't want her to. She relaxed against him and made a sound that was not quite a moan yet was soft and edged with need.

Almost no contact between them, yet his blood pounded in his ears. Their first time had been like this. Needful. Soul shattering. He burned in the moment, in her, in the heat of having his arms around her again. Familiar. Blazingly alive. She felt good in his embrace. Right. For the first time in years, he was whole.

She rested a hand on his upper arm, light at first, then fingers gripping. It was sweet, the way she leaned against him, sweet in his arms, and he wanted her so badly, he hurt. Jesus, she felt good, and he'd been too long without sexual satisfaction because he was imagining doing a good deal more than her practically chaste kiss.

That condition could not and did not last, a kiss that did not reflect the tension zinging between them. In the initial days of their relations, they'd kissed for hours, what seemed like hours, before he'd brought himself to touch a hand to more than her cheek. It wouldn't be the same now. Couldn't be. The soul-stealing pleasure of his first time was just that. First. And therefore memorable. He knew about women, now, thank you very much.

Even during that year between, he'd known how the world worked. So had Portia. They knew what it meant for her to be Portia and him to be the future Northword. He'd been to bed with her, they'd been lovers, and in his thoughts, he was already imagining sexual relations with her.

There was nothing innocent about his desire. Nothing at all. There never had been, not since that long ago day he'd realized his feelings for Portia were more than friendship. Not since the day he realized she felt the same.

She kissed him again, her lips parted this time, and he took what she offered. Somewhere in the back of his head he had the thought that she hadn't opened her mouth in order to invite more from him, but to draw breath. At the exact same time this was flitting through his thoughts, his mouth was open, too, and he was kissing her without restraint. Not in the least politely. Her mouth softened underneath his, matching, accepting him, answering him.

He knew a great deal more about kissing than he had ten years ago, but he was trembling just as he had then. They fit together, the two of them. He was taller since the last time she'd been in his arms, but she was still a good height for him, and she still made his heart too big for his chest.

The next thing he knew, the last of his restraint melted away, and he had her pressed against the stone wall of the archway, her head between his hands, his tongue in her mouth. Desperate for her. Desperately aroused. She kissed him back, her fingers gripping his upper arms in order to bring him closer. Familiar heat spiraled through him.

This.

He wanted *this.*

He rested his pelvis against her, and yes, he was hard, and that seemed exactly how things ought to be. He filled his fingers with her wet hair and sent his hat tumbling to the flagstones. He pulled back so her head was at a better angle.

Lust rattled him, shook away everything but the two of them. All his adult life, he'd missed this immersion of his senses, and he was not, not going to let this pass without living every minute and second.

In the moment after their mouths separated, she gasped, a groan of desire that laid waste to his lingering reservations. The breath left his body. Whatever this said about his character, he wanted Portia to come undone. As a point of pride to prove to her she'd been wrong to let them end. He wanted her to fall under his spell, to believe in her soul that no other lover would do but him. He pulled back, just his upper body and not much of that. Enough to kiss the rain from her cheeks and watch her eyes open. Unfocused and half-drunk with the same passion that filled him.

She set her palms on either side of his face and said, so softly the tremor in her words barely registered, "How I've missed you."

Yes. The word roared through him.

This.

He reached blindly past her and found the top of the nearest stable door. He fumbled it open and had just enough of his brain functioning that he thought to snatch a blanket hanging from a peg on the wall and spread it over the straw. Everything at Wordless was at the ready for the Viscount to make use of his long-neglected estate: clean blanket, clean straw. Thank God.

They dropped onto the blanket in a tangle of limbs and lips and, even, laughter. His lower back hit the blanket, and she was right here, kneeling between his upraised and spread apart knees. Her focus on him sent his heart pounding, and he propped one hand on the blanket and pushed up to loop an arm around the back of her neck and bring her in for another long, carnal kiss.

Outside, the rain beat down on the roof and cascaded onto the flagstones. All that faded away. There was no more cold. No rain. Nothing but the two of them. She offered her mouth. He accepted wholeheartedly.

With his free hand he adjusted their position so she straddled his hips. Kissing her still, he worked his hand underneath her skirts, pushing away damp-to-wet handfuls of that awful pink gown and her underskirts. She gave him the access he wanted.

His fingertips slid along her thighs, then up to cover her sex. Her pubic hair was as sparse as ever, almost nothing there. He pushed a finger between her legs. Slippery wet for him. Her gaze locked with his when his searching fingers slid along her. He knew how to touch her. He'd learned her. Memorized her. And he was better at this now. He was a much better lover than he had been. She set her hands on his shoulders and surrendered to her body.

"I missed you," she said again. "I thought I would die from missing you."

"Good."

She swallowed hard just once, a reaction that echoed through her body as she opened to him. He dropped into a sensual haze. Everything aroused him, from the slide of his fingers on her, the sound of her sigh that turned to a moan, his anticipation of what would come.

While he kissed her, tongue in her mouth, tasting and taking, he found the core of her and that particular spot that would bring on a build to unbearable tension. She groaned when he backed off, and her eyes snapped with frustration. He gave her a smug grin because she knew what he was doing to her and why. He laughed before he licked a trail of raindrops from her cheek and moved his fingers in her. So tight. She tensed, and he waited for her to relax.

"Has there been no one since me?"

Her eyes slowly focused. "I wasn't waiting for you, if that's what you mean."

He pushed his fingers farther into her, into that soft, tight heat. "We can argue about that later. Right now—"

"God, Crispin." The words came from her throat in a rush as she bowed toward him, hands pressed on the top of his shoulders, hips rocking into his palm cupping her sex. He watched her, felt her passage clench on his fingers.

There wasn't a damned soul anywhere near so he had the rare, great pleasure of neither one of them having to be in the least discreet. He thought he might have one more chance to pull her from the brink before she came, but her fingers dug into his shoulders, and she left him to fall off the cliff he'd constructed with her, her breath shuddering. He stroked, pressed, and she threw her head back and completely, utterly, with heartrending passion, surrendered to pleasure.

She belonged to him. He felt her tighten around his fingers, and he damn near lost all restraint, he wanted inside with such ferocity. He sailed beyond lust, beyond arousal. Exactly as it had been with them every time before. Despite the words he'd never written to her, he'd bared his soul to her in his letters and kept her close in so doing. He had indulged in a fantastically ironic game of revenge. He'd wanted her to know exactly what she'd given up and to regret that for the rest of her life.

"This is what we're like." The words rasped from his throat while she was still coming down from her climax, her head bowed to his shoulder. "You and I. It's not like this with anyone else. Just us."

While she clung to him, and he stroked away the last spasms of her pleasure, he used his other hand to unfasten his coat and the fall of his breeches and free himself from his clothing. With one last stroke along the folds of her body, he slid his palm to the curve of her backside and brought her up and toward him, and when his cock was at her entrance, she lifted her head and caught her lower lip between her teeth as she answered his upward thrust with the lowering of her hips.

An inarticulate sound burst from him. Heat. Slick dampness. Tight, almost too tight. She didn't relax around him because she'd not done this with anyone but him. He held back his urge to push hard. Slow at the start was good, too.

For a suspended moment, he was immersed in the simple pleasure of having his cock in a woman, but around the edges of that was this flicker of more. They weren't too young this time. This time, they were old enough to know there was nothing new in the world and that they did not invent passion, they created it between them, and it was *that* which was new and rare. He hissed as her body closed and softened around his cock. Nothing existed for him but her and his cock and the feral bliss of their connection.

"Crispin." She grabbed his shoulders and angled her hips. Her breath stuttered. "My God, Crispin." Her head dropped back and, Lord, she softened around him just enough, and now he thrust the way he wanted, needed to. He leaned in to kiss her exposed throat. So tight around him, she gripped his cock, all of it, and with a shout that was part demand and part plea, he rolled her onto her back and let the imperative of sex take him.

She pushed her hips toward him and drew up her knees, and he shoved her skirts up higher, out of his way. That flicker of *more* stayed with him, and he closed his eyes to deny what that meant. Instead, he found the angles that made her groan with pleasure and the ones that sent him racing to orgasm.

Her body tensed, and he concentrated on bringing her again, the two of them partially on their sides, his hand between them, his mouth at the side of her throat, hard enough to leave a mark, kissing her until she cried out, and he felt the contractions of her passage around him. He remembered everything that had made her moan before, but he was caught up in their desperation, urged on by the sounds she was making, by the roll of her hips against his, the grip of her arms around him.

He planted his hands by her head and pushed up so he could watch her face and leverage the weight of his pelvis with his thrusts into her. More selfish this time, but then she wrapped her legs around his hips and rocked into him, and he didn't feel selfish at all.

His balls tightened, and he thrust into her harder. Hard enough, hard enough. So close, and then he was tumbling, soaring toward exquisite pleasure and then falling into it, and he had just enough presence of mind not to come inside her. Barely.

When he returned to his senses, he opened his eyes, but he was still in a sensual stupor and had few thoughts but those that centered around his physical repletion. He drank in her face and the warmth where their bodies still touched. Pelvis to pelvis, her thighs at his hips, his softening member between them.

The rain had stopped while they'd been lost in each other. She wound her arms around his shoulders, and then his head, and pulled him down for a searing kiss. Afterward, when he'd pushed up to get his weight off her, the fierce sadness in her eyes made his heart swell again.

Her fingers brushed his cheek, pushed away the damp. "We ought to go, my lord."

He loved the sound of that honorific, the way the words left her lips soft and intimate and offered him her submission and her possession of him. He needed a few more breaths before he trusted himself to speak, and then she did first.

"Before you catch your death." Her hand lingered at his cheek, and he turned his head to kiss her fingers. She snatched her hand away. "That tickles."

"I don't want to go." He nestled against her. "I'm perfectly warm." He drew her nearer and breathed in the scent of her body, of sex and the damp heat of them both. "I can think of ways for us to stay warm."

"Oh, we'll just live here, then. In the stable."

"It's my stable. We can do what we like here." She didn't know, he thought. She didn't know what this meant to him, how shocking it was to feel he was home after ten years at sea with nights spent dreaming of stripping her naked and burying himself inside her.

She gave him a push, but she was already retreating from him, and he didn't know how to bring her back. "Obstinate as ever, aren't you?"

"I haven't changed."

She looked away. "That's not so."

He dipped his head to her ear, nipped her there and said, "Except, I think my prick is bigger, don't you?"

That made her laugh, and then him, and that was just like them, to be bawdy and find it amusing, as if they were the only lovers ever to speak crudely to each other. She turned her head to his chest, shoulders still shaking. Well. It was a fine joke, wasn't it? He kissed her again and realized it wouldn't take much for him to be ready again.

She pushed at his shoulders. "We should go. It's late."

With a sigh, he pushed away and fumbled to get himself decently back into his breeches. When he'd done that, he helped her arrange her clothes, too, or would have except that she lay on the blanket with her hair beginning to dry and glint with indisputable red, and her pale legs exposed and her lower belly, too. He thought he'd never seen anything more beautiful than her sex. A bit of the old guilt nipped at him, and he embraced that, too. Fucking his friend's sister was wrong, but he couldn't bring himself to care at this moment. Not then and not now.

He set his palm on her thigh, and then on the inside of her thigh. He'd scraped her there during their frantic coupling. When he thought to look at her face, he found her watching him with eyes that killed him. He slid his fingers upward, covered her sex, and, still watching her face, slid a finger inside her, one then two. "I'm no green boy, now," he said. She was getting slicker, and his two fingers moved in her easily. "If we didn't need to get home, I'd prove that beyond your ability to speak."

She pressed her head back because he'd pushed his thumb between her folds and along the flesh there. Her breath caught, but she managed to say, "You could try."

"Anything for you, my love. Anything."

"What's this?" She put a hand on his breeches. "Are you rising to the occasion, sir?"

"I think I am."

And she gave him a wicked smile that melted him inside and made him forget about Magnus and the fact that she was going to be married, and he didn't stop her from unbuttoning the fall of his breeches nor say a word when she took him in hand and drew back his foreskin. "You once liked me very well on my knees."

"Yes." He sat up then stood and stared into her eyes and understood that this was to be their very last time. "Please."

He buried his fingers in her hair when she took him in her mouth, and he let her bring him that way and all the while he told himself that if she could walk away from this, then by God, so could he.

Afterward, they tidied up as best they could, at last feeling the cold and damp, and they headed for the Grange. The sky hadn't cleared, though it wasn't raining, and the ground was thoroughly soaked. Dozens of tiny puddles lurked in the thick grass and made the footing uncertain. At the stone fence, he lifted her over again and did not put her down as quickly as he should have. He leaned in and kissed her, hard and fast before he released her.

"Don't," she said. "Don't do this."

Since she knew the way, he followed her through the fields. The path was muddier than when he'd tromped through here heading the other way, and the clouds were getting that heavy look while the air turned colder and thicker. They gave up trying to keep themselves out of the muck and just trudged through the field.

He kept a hand around her waist because that was what a gentleman did when he was escorting a lady across treacherous terrain. Before he was quite prepared to return to reality, they were at the Grange. Fat drops of water hit them as they dashed for the front of the house, running now and laughing for no reason other than it seemed right. The very moment they reached the path to the door, the rain became another torrent.

At the door, Portia turned, face to the sky and thrust a fist into the air. "Curse you, god of rain, curse you!"

He fumbled with the door, and when he got the thing open he grabbed Portia's other hand and pulled her inside—and they were still laughing.

Until he turned around and saw Mrs. Temple standing in the foyer, a look of utter betrayal on her face.

Chapter Six

WITH FINGERS CLUMSY from the cold, Portia worked at the buttons of Crispin's greatcoat, so heavy on her shoulders. She didn't dare meet Eleanor's eyes. She couldn't bear to see that wide-eyed hurt again. She wasn't Eleanor's equal, not fit to be in the same room as her.

This time, she'd betrayed more than Crispin's and her brother's trust. She'd hurt Eleanor, who did not deserve that, and she'd betrayed Jeremy, the man she was supposed to marry. Again. She wanted to weep with the horror of how badly she'd failed.

Hob appeared at the top of the servant's staircase. He came to a full stop, eyes wide when he saw the condition the two of them were in. Both of them soaked to the skin, her in Crispin's hat and greatcoat, muddy shoes, and water dripping everywhere.

"Hob," Eleanor said in a light voice. God, what a brilliant performance. You'd never guess now, that her sister-in-law thought there was anything the least untoward about this. "Do help Lord Northword with his wet coat."

Hob bowed and said, as he went to Crispin, "I was about to walk out to find thee, Miss."

"As well you didn't. You'd have got drenched, too." She meant to match Eleanor's aplomb and failed miserably at that, too. A shiver cut short her attempt to wipe water out of her face. She'd hardly minded her wet clothes and hair before, but now she was miserable inside and out. She managed to get the greatcoat unbuttoned and off her shoulders. Hob took it from her without a word.

"What on earth possessed you to go outside in weather such as this?" Eleanor's smile was sweet, so sweet.

It was on the tip of her tongue to confess everything. Every horrible impulse, every awful, unworthy thought, and beg for forgiveness. She ought to confess all the ways in which she'd traded a few moments of bliss for her very soul, but Crispin plucked his hat off her head and dropped it on the table by the door, and her words went unspoken. "Before you take my coat, Hob, see to sending a maid to help Miss Temple out of her wet things, won't you?"

"Yes, milord."

"That won't be necessary." Eleanor gave a clear, silvery laugh, but Portia knew she'd forever tainted relations with her sister-in-law, and very likely Magnus, too. Eleanor smoothly transferred her attention from Hob to Crispin. "Do take his coat. Lord Northword will catch an ague if he leaves it on."

Crispin lifted a hand. "Well, now, Hob, I can hardly remove my coat in front of ladies, can I? I'll not be so indelicate." On the table, a damp ring formed around the brim of the hat, slowly spreading outward. "I'll need my valet directly, if you'll see to that as well."

"Aye, milord."

Portia could not summon Crispin's cheer nor Eleanor's sweetness. Every glance, every word flayed her to the bone. Eleanor might as well have been there at the stable block, watching Portia fall into sin.

"You were gone so long, Magnus was worried." Eleanor picked up Crispin's hat and handed it to Hob. He accepted it with a bow and headed for the stairs.

"We were caught in the rain," Crispin said easily.

"Quite a downpour. We were worried."

"Did you not hear or see how it came down, Mrs. Temple?" He turned partway to her so that half his back faced Portia. He spoke so gently. "Forgive me that, ma'am. I know how intensely you feel everything."

She set her fingertips over her heart. "I do, my lord."

"I know I would have worried had I been in your place and my sister-in-law had gone out in such weather."

"Yes, my lord. Precisely."

"There was nothing we could do but take refuge where we could."

"Which was?"

He spread his hands. Water dripped from his sleeves onto the floor. "As you can well imagine, no place very dry. There was a tree. Not a very big one, I'm afraid. Not so far from the creek at the back of your property."

"A tree."

"Yes. A tree."

It didn't matter what Crispin said, or what excuses he made, or how convincingly he was for any of it, Portia knew every word was a lie. Eleanor's expression remained calm and pleasant, but dread curled in the pit of her stomach. That smile lay so heavy on them, around them, between them, that she could not react in any way.

"Thank you, Lord Northword, for going after her."

"You're quite welcome, Mrs. Temple."

"My dear Lord Northword. You ought to change into some dry clothes." Portia felt horrible. Eleanor was a woman incapable of malice and accustomed to thinking the best of everyone, and here they were, deceiving her. "You'll take a chill if you don't."

Crispin set a hand on the back of Portia's shoulder, no longer the man who'd kissed her senseless. Not the man who'd made love to her in a way that obliterated the life she'd built without him. He'd retreated behind a pleasant facade, and she was unbearably aroused by him. "You as well, Portia."

She nodded, but Eleanor detained her with a hand to Portia's arm. Crispin bowed to them and headed for the stairs.

"You've no idea how worried Magnus was for you," Eleanor said.

"We were caught in the rain."

"I do not understand why you would go outside at all when you did not feel well. And to make Lord Northword chase after you." Eleanor's smile faded. "I cannot imagine what people will say when they hear the tale. It's bound to follow you, my dear."

"I was foolish. I'm very sorry for the inconvenience and your worry."

"I do hope you've learned your lesson about acting impetuously."

"I have, thank you."

Eleanor pushed her toward the stairs. "Go on, now. We can't have you catching your death, either."

Bridget, the maid she shared with Eleanor, was waiting for her when she entered her bedroom. The young woman clucked at her bedraggled state.

Portia stood where she was, her thoughts no place in particular. She was glad to be ministered to with no need to do anything but move as required to get her wet clothes off. The cold penetrated to her bones. Had that second rain washed away the smell of sex? Lord, she didn't even know if Crispin had come on her clothes or his.

The maid unhooked the last of the fastenings of Portia's gown. "You poor thing. You're soaked to the skin. What happened?"

"Lord Northword and I were caught in the rain." She pulled her arms out of the sleeves of her gown and was immediately caught up in another shiver. "We took refuge under a tree." She fixed an image of the stream in her head, as if doing so would make it true. "By the stream. Near where my brother likes to fish."

"So far from the house, Miss?"

"It rained so hard, we were drenched. There was sleet, too." That was true. There would have been sleet by the stream as well.

"And here you went out without a cloak. Goodness, why? Come closer to the fire, Miss."

"Thank you." She shivered again when Bridget stripped her of her petticoats and undergarments. The places where Crispin's early beard had rasped against her skin were livid against her bone-cold skin. The bruise his mouth had left on her throat, the scrape left by his clothes against the inside of her thigh. She'd not felt any of that at the time, but she did now. Her skin contained the residue of his mouth, his hands, and his cock, the sigh of his breath. Bridget would surely put the evidence of her deception before Eleanor. Ten years since her fall from grace, and she'd given up body and soul without a thought. She'd tried to love elsewhere. She truly had.

Wiped down, dried off, hair combed out, and her in dry undergarments, she came out of her dumb state when Bridget picked up the pink gown. "I'll be up half the night with this."

"Don't bother." She sank onto an armchair. For the life of her, she couldn't think what Crispin had done when he came to passion, other than she was sure he'd not come inside her. "It can wait."

"If I don't launder this right away, it will be ruined for certain."

"If it can't be saved, burn it."

"Oh, it's too pretty for that."

"Keep it, if you like. Whether it can be saved or not." She met the maid's astonished gaze head on and managed a smile. "The color suits you better than it does me."

"That's kind of you. Thank you, Miss." She scooped up the rest of the wet clothes and undergarments then whisked away the gown before leaving Portia alone.

With no one to distract her, her heart crumbled. Part of her soul had vanished when she and Crispin proved unable to make a future together. Today, she'd had him in her arms again, and she wasn't sorry for that. She wasn't. But she'd been left with a newer and more painful reminder of exactly what she'd given up ten years ago

Chapter Seven

THE BLOODY RAIN had stopped again. In Northword's room, with its rear-facing windows, the light shifted with the constant change in the gaps of sky between the clouds. He held the note Hob had just delivered to him. He itched to toss it onto the fire. "No answer, Hob. Thank you."

He left it to his valet to give Hob a coin, which was quickly and discreetly done. The moment the door closed, he crumpled the note—predictably, the sheet was scented—and threw it on the dressing table. It landed half on the portable secretary he'd brought with him and half on the abandoned leather strop. *Meet at his earliest convenience.* The devil he'd be summoned like he was a misbehaving son. Not again.

He yanked on his shirtsleeve. "Are we finished with this nonsense yet?"

"No, milord." His valet was even tempered, thank goodness, since at the moment, Northword wore nothing but a shirt and clean breeches.

"Get on with it."

After that display of impatience and having to endure the arrangement of the rest of his clothes, he fussed more than usual with his appearance. He wanted to strike just the right note of lordly perfection before he went downstairs to face the wife of his closest friend. He was prepared to answer any and all charges laid at his feet. He would not give honor short shrift. Not ten years ago, and not now. He studied his reflection and decided, just this once, that his resemblance to his father was acceptable. His father had been a ruthless, heartless specimen of manhood.

He went downstairs to the parlor, reminding himself that he could not blame the woman for being concerned about Portia. The truth was, he *had* done precisely what one imagined happened when a man ended up alone with a woman. He half expected Magnus to be there waiting to accuse him, too, but he wasn't.

Mrs. Temple was just lifting a dish of tea to her lips when he walked in. She raised her eyes and smiled, and there was no anger in that smile, not the least sign of disapproval. He lifted a hand when she rose. He remembered the expression on his father's face when he had been called to account. His father had not smiled. "Please, don't stand on my account."

"Lord Northword. Thank you for coming downstairs so quickly." Mrs. Temple stood and curtseyed, unnecessarily deep if you asked him. He wasn't the damned Prince Regent. "Tea?"

"Yes, thank you." There was a tray of chevron-shaped shortbread on the table and two plates. The one before her had one of the familiar chevrons on it. The shortbread at Northword House had always been shaped thus.

She poured for him without asking his preference and moments later handed him a cup of tea adulterated with more milk than tea, for God's sake. She gazed at him with that guileless, ravishing smile of hers, and it did absolutely nothing for him.

He took the cup and set it down. He did not care for milk in his tea. Sugar only for him. "Thank you."

"Tea is so much more healthful when one drinks it with milk."

He helped himself to the sugar only to have her tap the table by his teacup. "My father's physician instructed him to take a cup every morning, prepared just so. Without sugar."

"Indeed?" She meant well. She did. A wisp of steam curled from the surface of his tea cup. He dropped in three lumps and then, in a moment of childish rebellion that was far too satisfying, added two more just to watch her horror. "It's not my habit to take milk with my tea."

She blinked several times, and his immediate instinct was to backtrack. She was not the sort of woman to see nuance in word or deed. "You ought to, my lord. After your adventures in our weather today, extra consideration for your health is in order, don't you agree?"

"I enjoy excellent health."

"Who's to say it will stay that way?" Her hand fluttered around her upper chest. "Why, just today you were caught in a storm and soaked to the skin. I shouldn't be astonished at all if you took ill as a result."

He took stock of his state and decided he was mildly offended and feeling decidedly manipulated by that wide-eyed look of incipient distress. "Thank you for considering my longevity."

"You're welcome, my lord." She beamed at him, and such was his irritation over tea with milk, he had almost no regret for his ironic tone. Besides, she gave no sign whatever that she'd heard the edge in his reply. "It was no trouble at all. I think you'll find you'll quickly acquire a taste for milk with your tea."

"I daresay you mean I shall learn to like a bit of tea with my milk." He laughed and smoothed out the emotion that had sparked his pointed response. He failed, for the bite remained. Was he not better than this? This was not a woman of subtlety, and it was not kind of him to behave so with her.

Her eyebrows drew together, and she tipped her head to one side. Portia, he thought, would have laughed out loud. But then again, Portia would have known better then to put milk in his tea. He sipped the concoction, and her smile turned incandescent. "Well?"

Undrinkable swill. He forced a smile because, after all, he would not hurt her feelings for the world.

"I'm glad you like it." She drank some of her tea. "I don't know what to make of this weather," she said. "It's March, nearly April, yet goodness. As cold and wet as December."

"Is it?"

"What plans have you for the remainder of the day, my lord?"

He put off the necessity of speech by taking a bite of shortbread. "This and that."

She tilted her head and smiled cheerfully. Beautiful woman, sublimely so. But she was married to Magnus Temple, and in so far as his physical tastes went, he'd never been partial to blondes. At the moment, he couldn't conceive of taking any woman besides Portia to bed. If he were to have that choice again. If there were any hope of repairing the break between them. Which there was not.

"I thought I'd walk out with Magnus later. To Up Aubry for a pint." He glanced out the window where there was now not a sign of a rain cloud. "If the weather holds as it looks to be doing. Improves the health, a good brisk walk."

"Oh dear." She folded her hands on the table. "I'm afraid Mr. Temple is not likely to be back from West Aubry in time for that."

He selected a piece of shortbread before he responded. "I didn't know he meant to go."

"He had parish business to attend to."

"Nevertheless, he should return in ample time."

"It's quite a long ride to West Aubry and back."

"By the road, yes. But he'll have walked. With the weather like this, he shan't be delayed for anything but his business."

"Oh, but he did not walk. He rode."

"Why would he ride?" By the road under these conditions, West Aubry was at least two hours distant.

"He would have had to walk through your private lands."

"Yes. And?"

"Enclosed lands. I've told him not to presume upon your good graces when that walk takes him within sight of your house."

He frowned. "He's always done so. Walked past Wordless—"

"Oh, I cannot approve."

"Of what? Magnus taking the shortest route to West Aubry?"

"There are a great many things of which one cannot approve." Her tone of voice gave him an unpleasant shock, for he'd begun to believe he would escape an uncomfortable conversation about him and Portia.

She gave him another ravishing smile. "Forgive me, but your estate, my lord, is Northword Hill. Not Wordless. It's not respectful of anyone to call it that. I've told Mr. Temple he mustn't. Portia, too, though she hardly listens to a word I say."

"Why, when I don't mind?" He put down his half-eaten shortbread. "Call the place what you will, Northword Hill, Wordless, or that 'moldering pile of stones'—your husband has always had leave to walk through the property. Even when my father was alive."

She smiled as if she knew a secret and did not intend to share.

"I've no issues with him or anyone from the Grange continuing to do so."

"It's a matter of what's proper, my lord." She got that lost look again, and it did tug at his heart. He resisted the urge to comfort her. "A man of Mr. Temple's position and station in life, who has dedicated himself to the work of God, cannot be seen by his parishioners to act in any way that is improper." She dabbed at her mouth. How did Portia endure this without going stark raving mad? "That holds true for all his family. All we Temples must be above reproach. His wife and his sister included."

He ate his shortbread without tasting any of it while he marshaled his thoughts and temper. Surely, he thought, she did not mean to be so officiously and stupidly nice about Magnus doing what he had always done, and with his blessing. And surely it was only his guilty conscience that made him think she was working her way toward a condemnation of him being out in the rain with Portia. In the stable block with their clothes undone or tossed up, neither of which facts she could possibly know.

"I think, Mrs. Temple, that your distinction is too fine."

She plucked another chevron of shortbread from the tray and ate it slowly. "When we fail to observe the niceties, we court the danger of failing in our larger responsibilities. To God, to ourselves, and to others." He could practically hear Magnus speaking through her words. "Does not the Bible tell us to respect our elders and those who are in a position superior to us? As those who are our superiors must be mindful of what is best for those beneath them in rank and consequence."

"I'll grant the inhabitants of Doyle's Grange an easement to cross the estate lands." He shrugged. "I'll write to my solicitor and have it done."

"Until then. . ."

He was so desperate to put off the looming unpleasantness that he changed the subject with an utter lack of tact or finesse. "I've known Magnus and Portia since I was a boy. We have always been on the best of terms. I should hope you believe there's little I would not do for either of them."

She leaned forward. "Magnus and I are so very grateful for all that you have done for us. He would never ask you for anything on his own, you understand. He is too fine a man for that."

He nodded.

To his astonishment, her eyes filled with tears. "He will not ask you; so I shall."

"Please." He could not help thinking that he'd been maneuvered to a point where he'd agree to almost anything to keep from seeing her dissolve into tears.

"He's worked so long and hard, and for his own beloved sister to thwart him like this." She picked up her napkin and dabbed at her eyes.

"I don't understand."

"This marriage of hers."

"What of it?"

"Mr. Stewart is a fine man. We all adore him." She fisted a hand on the table and looked so distressed, he wasn't certain if he should hand her his handkerchief or call for a servant to bring a vinaigrette. "Even if Portia were as madly in love with Mr. Stewart as I am with Mr. Temple, the fact is, her marriage does nothing to secure Magnus's future.

A chill went down his spine, and his heart skipped a beat. "She's not in love with him?"

"Oh, I'm quite sure she has tender feelings for him, my lord." She smiled sadly. "Who would not? He is delightful. But she is not a woman of such pure emotion as I am. Surely, you have noticed this small defect in her."

"I have not."

"She does not feel as I do. Nor love so deeply. I have observed that few people do." She waved a hand. "A marriage between her and Mr. Stewart is of no advantage to Magnus at all."

He floundered, torn in too many directions to make sense of this. He'd come downstairs convinced he would be pressured to marry Portia, that it was only a matter of time before Magnus confronted him, and instead, unless he was badly mistaken, he was being asked to interfere in Portia's engagement. "What is it you would have me do?"

No artist in the world could resist the temptation to paint her smile onto a Madonna. "Convince her to come to London before she ties herself irrevocably to a man who does not suit her. Put the full weight of your approval behind our appearance there with her. Any number of gentlemen of good family would be pleased to marry an attractive woman. You've not noticed that Portia is quite a lovely woman, but I assure you it's so. With the proper gowns and only a little more attention to her appearance, why, she cannot help but make an impression."

As it turned out, he did not need to concoct a reply to that, for she continued talking.

"A pretty woman whose family has the friendship of Lord Northword? Any of them would be men who could do Magnus more good, and suit her much better than Mr. Stewart."

"Have you someone in mind?"

She brightened. "Several candidates, as a matter of fact." She counted off on her fingers, but the names went by in a blur.

"So many?"

"Naturally, there are one or two at the top of my list, my lord. I understand it is a great favor to ask you to introduce suitable men to her, but consider that Magnus might one day be a Bishop. Why, he might aspire to York or even to Canterbury. It's not beyond his abilities." She leaned in, intent. "If his sister makes a marriage of no advantage? All I ask is that you make known your approval of her when we are in London. What could be happier for us all?"

Chapter Eight

Ten past midnight

PORTIA DIDN'T MOVE from her chair when someone tapped on her door. With Crispin here, they were keeping later hours, and after all, she wasn't in bed yet. She pulled her shawl tighter around her shoulders but kept her legs drawn up on the chair. She wore only her chemise and the night wrapper she'd had since she was thirteen. Her hair was still loose even though by now it was dry. One had to expect that a woman who'd taken refuge in her room might not be dressed.

Whoever it was tapped again. In the best case, her visitor was Eleanor. In the worst case, Magnus himself had come to confront her. Either way, the visit could only be about her and Crispin. "Come in."

The curtains weren't drawn. Portia, seated in an armchair halfway between her dresser and the fireplace, continued to stare at the glass. On this clear, cold night with the stars shining bright in the sky, she could just see the moonlit branches of the rowan tree she'd planted. Already, the slender branches looked stronger. Decades from now, her tree would provide shade for whoever lived here. The door opened and cast a slice of light on the windows. Instead of the rowan tree or the stars, she saw a reflection of the door.

With a click, the door closed. She had no need to look; she knew who it was. A moment later, the key turned in the lock. Her skin rippled with awareness during the brief silence that followed that sound. He put his lantern on the table beside the door. "The walls aren't blue anymore."

"I decided I liked this better." She stood but stayed beside her chair, her back to the window now, one hand resting along the top curve of the chair.

Out of habit, she thought of all the times Crispin had been here. At night. When he ought not to have been and when the walls had been a pale blue. With them breathless and giddy. She gestured. "Moss. This green is called moss. Darker than the parlor, but green nevertheless and very much underappreciated, I do assure you. Except by me. It seems I overappreciate the color."

He laughed and looked around the room, taking it in. "I like it."

Her fingers dug into the chair. He took up all the space. All the air. "I was expecting Magnus or Eleanor."

"To take you to task, I presume."

She nodded.

"I am the hero of this tale, you know. The knight in shining armor facing down the dragon. Did you not hear your sister-in-law praise me for rescuing you from a storm you were obstinate enough to be out in?" He wandered into the middle of the room and took up even more space. She turned with his progress. "I've already been thanked, so you needn't add yours."

"I was not in need of rescue."

"No?" He looked around again. "Other than the walls, everything's the same."

She made a fist of her hand. "What are you doing here?"

His smile vanished. "She wishes me to join in her efforts to get you to London before you are married."

"Oh. Oh dear. My apologies for that."

"Shall I?"

She looked down and scratched an eyebrow. "It's awful the way she gets what she wants, isn't it?"

"Thoroughly unsettling."

"Don't abet her in this or any other scheme."

He nodded once, and into the growing tension he said, "We should talk. About what happened at Wordless." His voice was so brisk, he hardly sounded like the man she knew. His voice turned him into a stranger, into the Viscount Northword, not a man she'd known nearly her entire life. Not the man who'd been her first lover and her most recent one, but a stranger of terrible consequence.

She stared at her hand on the top of the chair and forced herself to uncurl her fingers. "I'm not sure there's much to say."

He walked to her dresser so that she had to turn around to face him. He'd stood exactly there dozens of times before. There was no mistaking him for the seventeen-year-old he'd been. He'd grown into all the promise of his manliness and gained an air of command. Both things suited him. "I think we ought to talk, don't you? Clear the air." He scratched his head. "Of all that."

"Why? I don't regret it."

"Nor I."

She couldn't tell if Crispin was pleased or not and so said nothing.

He continued. "Please be perfectly clear on that point. I don't regret what happened either. Even though it ought not to have happened."

"I don't think men regret such encounters." Force of habit put a lilt in her voice. She wasn't used to being on edge with Crispin, and here, in her room, their old familiarity seemed especially close.

"Is that all it was to you?" Of all the items on her dresser, he picked up one of the few new ones to be found. The porcelain pot no bigger than her fist contained as many crocuses as she could fit in it. A crease appeared between his eyebrows. "An encounter."

"I'm sorry if that's inaccurate." Briefly, she closed her eyes. Her memories of him took on weight, the nights he'd walked here from Wordless under a starlit sky like tonight's. "I don't know what it was to you."

"We'll leave it at that, then." He turned and tilted the pot, watching the play of light over it. He wore a thick gold ring on his first finger, and that, too, was something she did not recognize. In ten years, she'd acquired only two pieces of jewelry: a necklace and a pair of earrings, both a gift from Magnus when she turned twenty-one. Since she'd almost immediately lost one of the earrings, she almost never wore the necklace that matched. "You were not your usual self," he said in his stranger's voice. He looked up. "It would not be absurd to suggest I took advantage. I'll apologize if you need that from me."

"No."

He leaned against the dresser, still holding the pot of crocuses. "Your favorite flower."

"They've always reminded me of you." Too late, she realized how much that gave away. "They bloom every spring in the field between Northword Hill and the Grange. Every spring when Magnus and I were little, I tried to count them whenever we walked up the hill."

He gave her a sideways look. "I remember."

"There weren't as many then as there are now. The first spring after you left, the hill was covered with crocuses as far as the eye could see." She waved a hand. "Not just a few, but a carpet of them. People came all the way from Aubry Sock to see them. I told Magnus to paint it for you. Did he not send it on?"

"He did. My wife saw it and thought it lovely." He let out a short breath. "I didn't know it was from you. I had it framed and gave it to her as a gift."

"Did you?"

"You know Magnus. He's a gift for choosing an interesting perspective in whatever he paints or draws. She particularly liked that you could see a part of Wordless. I suppose it's still hanging in her room." Crispin, slouched against her dresser, set the pot back in its place. He watched her under half-lidded eyes. A lock of his hair, that lovely shade that was not quite blond yet not quite brown either, fell in a crescent slash across his forehead. "It's a wonder you don't curse them the way she does."

He meant Eleanor. "Never." She brought her shawl closer around her shoulders and caught the edge of his frown. "Why would I?"

"I don't know." He shrugged and avoided looking directly at her by focusing his gaze just past her ear. "Because I took your virginity on a night like this?"

"Turnabout is fair play. After all, I took yours."

That frown of his flashed again. He ought to have smiled at her joke, but he didn't. And this time, he looked her full in the face. "For whatever offense I gave that made you leave me."

She sat on the armchair, just on the edge of the seat, and clutched the padded arm. Her heart turned to ash in her chest while she searched for the words to explain what had happened. "I didn't leave you."

"You didn't come with me." He made a sharp, dismissive gesture. "It was ten years ago. We were practically children. Young and foolish, the both of us, but I have always, always, wanted to tell you that I never wavered." He set his palm on his head and looked away in a gesture she'd seen a thousand times from him. When he did that, he was gathering his words, assembling thoughts, so that when he spoke he said precisely what he meant to say. "It's done. You and I. Over."

"I know." She wanted to go to him, but that would be worse than presumptuous. She wanted to badly to touch him, to tell him she understood his anger and that he should let old hurts go.

"I ought not blame you for youth and inexperience of life, and yet I do." He let out a frustrated breath. "It's nonsense, my doing that. But seeing you again—Sometimes, I think we were only yesterday and all my old habits with you come back."

"It's been difficult for me, too."

He pushed away from the dresser and walked to the fireplace. For a while, he stood with his back to her, staring at the line of chimney ornaments on the mantle. He touched a bird's nest he'd given to her when she was eleven. "You still have this."

"I'm sentimental about such things. Magnus is always on about how I refuse to discard anything. I've collected a box of buttons I'll surely never use. Old grammars and the like. Sketches Magnus did when he was a boy. I kept them all, you know."

He turned, and his eyes were hard as stone. "What happened today should not have. I'm sorry. I hope you'll forgive me."

"There's nothing for me to forgive."

He said, softly, after far too long, "I think about him all the time."

She closed her eyes.

"He'd be nearly ten, if you'd had a boy. I imagine him with your beautiful eyes. My mouth." His voice rasped over her, killing her. "Or a girl with your hair and my smile. She might have had your brother's gifts."

"Don't."

"I don't think I ever told you how I felt, and I ought to have."

She turned her head toward him. "It's not the men who suffer. It's the women who are turned out of the house. Women bear all that burden."

"How could you not trust me? The day you told me you were with child, that night, I lay in my bed at Wordless, and I was glad, and at the same time I was afraid of what my father would say when I told him. Afraid of Magnus and what he'd think of me for what I'd done to you. And afraid for you. Terrified for what might happen to you."

She didn't dare open her eyes. She couldn't, didn't, and still the tears came. In those days when she'd been trapped and desperate and unable to tell anyone for fear Magnus would find out, she'd felt as if the poison of Lord

Northword's hatred had given the man the power to twist the world into any shape he wished. Crispin's father did not wish for a world where his son married a woman like her, and he had transformed the world until he had what he wanted.

"I knew you were afraid and distraught and that you blamed yourself, as if you'd gotten with child without any help from me. I knew you blamed yourself, but I never told you how much I wanted to marry you and hold our baby in my arms. I thought you understood that. I thought you knew I loved you too much to let that happen to you or our child."

She rested her head on her arm, face down so that she could not see him. "Don't do this to me."

He moved closer. "What, Portia? Do what?" The ice was back in his voice. "You went to that woman without giving me a chance to convince you I would do anything you needed. Anything. My father could threaten me all he liked, and I would not have refused to marry you. You didn't need to save yourself from that fate."

The enormity of her loss hit her again. What might have been, the life they might have had. Words came on the heels of a short, low breath, fast and propelled by the force of all the years she'd kept those words back. She lifted her head and stared at him through a blur of tears.

"Your father told me if I married you, he'd have Magnus expelled from school. He said if you were still a minor he'd have the marriage annulled. He told me if I thought we could wait until Magnus was graduated, that if we did that, Magnus would never have a living anywhere, not for as long as he lived. He told me he'd already personally seen to it that the Royal Academy would never admit him, and he had. He did that to punish me, to make sure I knew he'd stop at nothing. That's why Magnus was rejected. If it weren't for me, he would have been admitted. He ought to have been."

He set both hands to his head this time and stared past her.

"Your father was right about me. And so are you. I didn't love you enough to bring more harm to my brother. I couldn't do that to him when I'd already cost him his dream."

Crispin dropped his hands to his side. She didn't move. The silence ripened. At last, he said, "You ought to have told me."

She leaned sideways against the chair and stared at the window frame past Crispin's shoulders. She didn't want to know if he was looking at her. It would kill her to know. "What difference does it make what I should have done or wish I had? There's only the choice I made. And I am sorry. So sorry to have hurt you. I never wanted that."

"I married someone else, and by the time I understood what an awful mistake I'd made marrying in anger and resentment, it was too late." His voice was bleak, and if there had been a way to blot that out, she would have. "My wife deserved better. She was a good and decent woman, and she deserved more from her husband than the man she got."

That took her aback enough to look at him. She had always imagined they were happy. Crispin would never have married a woman who wasn't worthy of him. "I'm sorry."

"Don't be."

He made a face when she reacted by reaching to him. Her hand fell back to her lap. "Don't you be either, Crispin Hope. You never wrote of her except in the most tender and respectful ways. I always thought it was plain as anything that you loved her very much indeed."

"Not the way I loved you."

"Of course you didn't." She clenched her hand on her lap. "There isn't only one way to love someone."

He strode to her and did not stop moving until she was trapped between him and the chair. Her heart headed toward her toes. His every look recalled what they'd done today, and though she still felt the aches of their encounter, her body wanted him again. She wanted all the marks of their passion, the imprint of him on her soul rising up and taking shape once again. "Then why do I feel as if nothing's changed with us?"

"The past hasn't changed. It's there in our memories. It won't ever go away."

The silence was uncomfortably long.

"I loved you."

"We can't go back." She wiped at her tears. "My God, can you imagine if we tried? We aren't that couple anymore. I don't know you any more than you do me. Please, let's be friends. Let's keep that."

He stepped back.

Her heart broke again.

Chapter Nine

Two days later

AFTER BREAKFAST THEY were all sitting in the parlor as near to the fire as they dared now that Hob had brought in the morning post. There were letters for everyone. Crispin had several, most of which he put in his pocket, but he read aloud from one in which a friend of his, a man whose name she recognized from reading the *Times*, described with lively detail his days spent hiking in Northumberland.

Magnus sat on a chair idly sketching while Eleanor knit. When Crispin had finished reading his letter and they had exchanged news or excerpts from the other correspondence, Portia cleared her throat and said, "I have happy news."

Eleanor put down her knitting and beamed at her. "I adore happy news, and I should very much like to hear yours."

"Jeremy and I have advanced the date of our wedding."

In the silence that followed, Eleanor drew her eyebrows together. "But the day's been set for weeks now."

"We've decided to be married sooner. Not October, Eleanor, but May."

"May? Next year, do you mean?"

"No. Next month. Nothing fancy. There's no time for anything but the simplest of ceremonies, and we've decided we prefer it that way."

Eleanor's hands stilled. "But May is when we'll be in London. For the end of the Season."

"You and Magnus may still go, of course."

"When did you decide this?"

"I wrote to Mr. Stewart just a few days ago." She was aware of Crispin's silence, the way he watched her. "He agreed a May wedding was more convenient than October. I should like it very much, Magnus, if we could be married here at Doyle's Grange on the last Sunday in May. As soon as the last of the banns are called."

Eleanor's hands fluttered. "I've told everyone you're to be married in October. In West Aubry."

Her stomach folded in on itself. She glanced at her brother, hoping to see in his face confirmation that he supported her in this change. Magnus did not meet Portia's eyes.

Eleanor smiled radiantly. "You see? It's not convenient at all. I assure you, I am happy to be of assistance in bringing your wedding about in a suitable manner. At a suitable and convenient time."

"Jeremy and I are settled on this."

"I excel at managing such matters."

"I'm sure you do."

She leaned close and gave Portia's arm a squeeze. "Your parents would have wanted you to have a lovely wedding, attended by the people you love. You've not had a mother's firm guidance nor been able to see your father's pleasure at seeing you properly married. The way I saw how happy mine were when Magnus and I were married."

Resentment bubbled up even as she told herself that Eleanor only wished for her wedding to be perfect. But she wanted nothing more than to be gone from Doyle's Grange. She did not want to continue an intruder on her brother's new life. She wanted to be away from a world where the Viscount Northword could destroy her peace of mind. "I appreciate that. Truly, I do." Lord, she could feel Crispin's gaze. "But Jeremy and I are in accord that this change in date is for the best."

"You have a sister now, my dear. Wiser and more experienced in such matters. I'll take care of everything. You ought to be married in the church at West Aubry, with your brother presiding. You can't have seen my guest list, the people I've invited for October. Or Mr. Stewart's guests for that matter. I have the list from his mother, you know."

"Have you?"

"With your brother so newly established in his living, you would be very selfish to insist on being married anywhere but in West Aubry. Will you deny his parishioners the sight of their spiritual leader living by example what he preaches to them every Sunday? No, my darling Portia, they deserve to see his sister married in their church, by the man who guides them spiritually."

Magnus cleared his throat. "I think I can as well see my sister married here as at West Aubry."

"But, my dear." She blinked several times.

Portia cast about for anything to stop the tears that threatened. "Magnus is so new to his living, and you have so many expenses just now. The Grange, the work at the vicarage. I don't wish for there to be any fuss. It's not as if I'm a young bride. No, no, Eleanor, I must decline all that, despite your generous offer of assistance. We shall have a small ceremony attended by family only."

Crispin leaned forward, and Portia's stomach hollowed out. His hands had touched her, stroked her, and she wanted to hold the remembered sensations close. "The last Sunday in May, you say?"

"Yes, my lord." Portia wanted to kick him for reminding Eleanor of that. "I know you're to be back in London by then, but it's all settled." She held out a hand and smiled. "I accept your good wishes."

He did not take her hand or return her smile. "You cannot think for a moment that I would miss your wedding." Just now he reminded her so strongly of his father that she felt an echo of the dread she'd felt when in the presence of the late Lord Northword. "I wouldn't. Not for the world."

She allowed him to see her opinion of that. Magnus got up and put more coal on the fire, a welcome distraction, actually.

Crispin wasn't having any of it. "If I must rearrange a meeting or two, then I shall, and there's an end to it. I shall be here. The last Sunday in May."

This, then, was her way out. He'd given her the rope that would save her. "Thank you, my lord. How kind. It will mean a great deal to have you there."

Eleanor gave her a panicked look. "But Portia, the house is so very small. If you're to be married here, where will everyone stay? There's no place suitable for Mr. Stewart and his family to stay in Up Aubry, and Aubry Sock is too far away. As is West Aubry from the Grange. No, the wedding must take place where we can accommodate the people who will insist on being here." Her voice trembled. "Doyle's Grange is lovely. I adore it, but there is so little room for guests—and when it is in this condition. . .In West Aubry, there's the vicarage and several inns where guests might be made quite comfortable."

Once again, Crispin settled everything. "Your guests are welcome to stay at Wordless. There's plenty of time to open up the house, Mrs. Temple. I am happy to do so."

"Brilliant, Word. And generous. You see?" Magnus said to Eleanor. "It's settled as easily as that."

"Northword Hill is at your complete disposal." Crispin looked to Magnus. "You are not to be out of pocket for this, do I make myself clear? Whatever staff you hire will be employed by me. My valet will be more than happy to assist with the arrangements. I know Mrs. Temple will manage everything beautifully, and I shan't have to worry about a thing. Nor will Portia."

"Thank you, my lord," Portia said. She smiled with pure relief. "That is very kind of you to offer your home."

He waved a hand. "It's the least I can do." Then he gazed at Portia. "I look forward to meeting Mr. Stewart."

Chapter Ten

Three days later

PORTIA STOOD IN front of the lavender, scissors in hand. The rowan tree was to her right, leaves no longer drooping, just as Hob had foretold. She broke off one of the forming lavender blossom heads and rolled it between her fingers. Even this early in the season, the scent was lovely. Her heart pinched at the thought that she would not be here to see it in full bloom. Nor any of the rest of the garden.

Jeremy and his mother had arrived several hours ago, and after much ado, Mrs. Stewart was resting upstairs. Jeremy, Magnus, and Crispin were ensconced in the back parlor while Eleanor was driving the servants to distraction overseeing preparations for her and Magnus's departure for Brighton. Portia had escaped the chaos outside the moment at the first opportunity.

Boot heels clicked on the stone steps. Not her sister-in-law, thank God. Too fast to be Magnus. Her brother never walked when he could stroll nor hurried when he could walk. Hob never moved that quickly, either. Those footsteps came too quickly for anyone but Crispin.

She turned and saw him striding toward her in his tasseled Hessians and snug breeches. The lawn was muddy from the most recent rain, and he had to slow down, not much, but some, when he left the path to head her direction. When he reached her, she curtseyed and then, from deviltry, added, "Good afternoon, my lord."

He stopped in front of her seconds before she would have been required to move, if only to avoid being run over. He ended up too close. He'd walked out without a hat, which she found absurdly thrilling despite it being obvious he'd come here with his annoyance in tow. She stood her ground. Besides, two steps back, and she'd be standing in the lavender.

"Is that woman somewhere near?" He lifted a warning hand. "You know whom and what I mean. Can she see or hear us right now?"

"I don't believe so."

"Then don't curtsey." His mouth thinned. "It's not necessary. Not when it's just the two of us."

"You think not?"

"That hasn't changed." He jammed his hands into his coat pockets. He was splendid in high passion, and it made her sorry for the anger that zinged between them. "She isn't here to cry mock tears and convince us all she mustn't be upset lest she melt away in a puddle of grand emotion."

She crushed the bits of lavender in her free hand and let the bruised and torn pieces fall to the ground between them. "Why are you here?" She waved a hand. "Out here, I mean. Glaring at me as if I've gone into your room and mixed up all your papers. Or poured ink on your best shirts."

His mouth twitched down. "As if you couldn't guess."

"I can't."

He worked his jaw, and she was tempted to take a step back. She didn't, though. "What the deuce, Portia?"

"Don't scowl like that." Never mind that he was glaring at her, he was all bluster. Eleanor was inside the house and could not see them. With the side of her thumb, she smoothed away the furrow in his forehead. She had the private pleasure of seeing him struggle to master himself, and it made her feel better, knowing that he might be feeling as to sea as she did. "Did no one tell you your face will freeze in that expression?"

He took her hand and held it. "You can't be serious about this fellow."

She pasted on a smile, but that did nothing for the lurch in her chest. "I like his mother."

"A delightful woman, I grant you that." He'd always been scrupulous in that way, honest even when it would have been easier not to be. "I can't say I find her son equally delightful."

"Stop."

"Your face will freeze like that," he said.

"If it does, at least I shan't spend the rest of my life with an ogre's glower."

He burst out in laughter, and she tried not to and failed. "Imp."

"The largest imp there ever was." She curtseyed to him, and she almost, almost, felt as if all was well between them. It wasn't. It never could be, no matter how many times they fell into sin or avoided it.

"Portia." Crispin threw an arm wide. "Fifty if he's a day. I don't care how much you like his mother. What do you mean by this?"

She freed her hand from his and clasped her hands behind her back. She never had liked dealing with what people meant rather than what they were saying, and right now Crispin was not saying what he meant. "I don't understand what you're asking. *What do I mean by this?* What do *you* mean?"

"I'm not asking you anything."

"My mistake." She tapped her toe, and even though on the grass her boot made no noise, her irritation with him was plain enough.

"I'm demanding that you explain why you're marrying a man old enough to be your father."

"Sit, Fido," she murmured. "Good dog."

He took a step forward. "Don't make light of this. You don't love him. Don't insult me by telling me you do. I know when a woman's in love."

"I'm sure you do." And that came out too hard and too resentful.

"Mrs. Temple is right. You don't love him."

She set free her hands to break off another stalk of lavender and tap his chest with it. "You're a worse bully than she."

"I've not bullied you since you were ten. You wouldn't stand for that from me." He flexed his fingers then crossed his arms and glared at her. "Do you love him?"

So much was already broken with her life, she did not wish to have it fracture now by telling him things she did not care to admit to herself. Before Crispin arrived, she had been at peace with her decision to marry; indeed, she had been near to desperate to leave Doyle's Grange, and the sooner the better. She reached behind her and broke off another stalk of lavender.

"The truth."

"We've discussed this until it's dead. Exploded."

When she looked at him again, he frowned at her. "No, we haven't. We haven't discussed this at all."

She stared at the crushed lavender on her palm. "Perhaps I don't wish to discuss it. There's nothing can be done."

"Did what happened at Wordless mean nothing to you? Is that what you'll have me believe?"

Guilt slid down her spine, but she ignored it. "Don't tell me what I feel. Or what I ought to do. Or think or decide about anything." She glared at him. "I am capable of making my own decisions, you know. I think I know what will make me happy."

He snorted, and that earned him a glare. "I demand an answer."

His curt words got her back up. "Do you, now?"

Being Crispin, he wasn't concerned with the sort of manners he used with Eleanor. "I do."

"What do you expect me to do about that?" In a fit of pique, she curtseyed. "My lord."

"Stop that. I've told you it's nonsense."

"No, it isn't. It isn't at all. Stop telling me it is."

"Portia." His attention was too much for her just now. That sort of attention. His looking at her the way he had at Wordless. "Please. Do you love him even a little? How am I to bear the thought of you marrying a man you don't love?"

She whirled away from him and the lavender, and walked away from the tree that was her permanent farewell to Doyle's Grange. He followed. Of course he followed. He never knew when to let well enough alone. She let out a breath. "I am weary of all this interference in my life. Yours *and* Eleanor's. If it continues any longer, I swear to you, I shall marry Jeremy tomorrow, and you and Eleanor can go to the devil."

"I'm not going anywhere with that woman. Besides, you can't. The banns haven't been read."

She snorted. "Scotland's not far."

His eyes pierced her, and she was sorry she looked because she couldn't forget the feel of him, the rightness of having her arms around him and her heart beating in her chest. He said, "You're too young to be marrying."

She stopped walking and stared at him, incredulous. "What?"

"You heard me."

Laughter bubbled up, and for her very life she could not keep it back. He was so ridiculously earnest. She managed to draw in a breath and suppress her mirth long enough to speak. "You ought to be mocked for uttering such an absurdity. Too young? Good heavens, you can't be serious. I'm twenty-seven. Better if you agree with Magnus and remind me at every turn that I am on the verge of too old to be marrying."

"You're not too old." He yanked his hands free of his pockets and gesticulated.

"You shan't find an answer in the air. Nor change my mind, either, not with all the bluster in the world."

"Bluster. I'm not blustering at you. And that isn't what I meant at all. You're too young to be marrying *that* man."

She folded her arms underneath her bosom and gazed at him, tapping one foot on the ground. He stared at her bosom. She looked too, brushing at her bodice. "Have I got something on me?"

He lowered his voice. "Come away with me again. To Wordless. Right now."

"No."

"Why not?"

She pointed at the house. "Because the man I mean to marry is inside."

"It didn't stop you before."

"I was upset. Not in my right mind. That shouldn't have happened. You said so yourself." She closed her eyes a moment and tried to put the ring of truth and conviction into her words. "It was habit. That's all. As you said, it's how we are. That doesn't make it right. It doesn't change anything."

"Meaning?"

"I can't stay here. It's impossible. With all"—she waved a hand—"that. Not even for you."

"For yourself. For God's sake, Portia." He ran his hands over the top of his head, leaving his hair in disarray. "I'll speak frankly, if you don't mind."

"Would you?" she said with full irony. "Just this once."

He threw one arm wide. "I thought the man was going to pull down my britches and kiss my arse."

She took a step away from him. "You don't have to marry him."

"Nor do you."

"Yes, I do."

Crispin opened his mouth to speak and then didn't, then blurted out, "What?"

Chapter Eleven

SHE WATCHED CRISPIN'S eyes get big, and she wasn't sure whether to laugh at him or be insulted when she realized what he was thinking. She put her hands on his chest and gave him a push. Anger was quite useful at times. It kept her from bursting into tears. "Is that what you think of me?"

"No."

"That I'm marrying him because of that?"

He refused to be budged. "Why else would a woman feel she has to marry a man?"

"I am not with child, Crispin Hope." She crossed her arms over her chest.

"I didn't say you were."

"You thought it." Her breath caught at the insult. "Go to hell."

"I'm convinced I shall. Why else would you marry that arse-kissing toady?"

"He's not." She made fists of her hands. "Because I want to."

"He is. Believe me, I have met my share of men like him." He crossed his arms, and he only did it to make himself seem bigger and more powerful. Well, she wasn't about to be cowed by him. "I don't believe you want to marry him. Not ten seconds after I met the man, I knew you couldn't possibly be in love with him. You're marrying him because you don't want to be here. There, I've said it."

"You certainly have." She bit off the words.

Crispin seemed to realize he'd spoken out of turn again, for he flushed. "I refuse to apologize for telling you I don't like him. Someone needs to tell you that you can do better."

Anger boiled up. She was speechless with it. And thank God, for she'd have said words she would surely regret.

He reached for her, but she stepped to the side, and he missed his target. "Don't marry him. You shan't be happy."

She tucked her hands behind her back and cocked her head. "Will you tell me whom I ought to marry? Please. I should like to know. There aren't many eligible men here. Men I'd want to marry, and it's been years since any unattached gentleman came to the Grange to ask my brother if an offer would be kindly received." She rocked on her heels. "The blacksmith is handsome enough, I suppose, but he's already got a wife. If you tell me to go to London and find a husband there, I'll never speak to you again. You and Eleanor can dry each other's tears over that."

He took her by the shoulders and stared at her. "I'm serious about this. He's not anything like your equal."

"You are not my father. Nor are you my brother. Nor anyone else with authority over me. How dare are you tell me not to marry a decent man?" She twisted away from him. "Under the circumstances, he's the best I can do."

"No, he isn't." He grabbed her upper arm and turned her to face him. "Look at me."

She thwarted him by staring at the sky. Amid the blue, the moon was a pale crescent, washed out by the late winter sun.

"You are a stubborn, stubborn woman. Look at me."

She did and ought not to have because the moment she did all her resentment evaporated.

"I've no authority over you, God knows that's so. But who else will you trust with the truth? Your sister-in-law? Or will you tell Magnus the reason you're marrying a man you don't love?"

"You know I can't." Tears burned in her eyes, and she had to look away to keep him from seeing how close she was to losing herself. She couldn't. She could not complain to her brother about his wife nor breathe a word about her unhappiness.

"Come here." Crispin tugged on her arm and spread his other arm wide and she walked into his arms where she had always been safe and where all was right with the world. "Tell me. You'll feel better for it; you know you shall."

"I've tried to like her. I've tried. And I can't." She rested her forehead on his chest. He smelled good, and his body was warm. "She's empty and shallow, and she loves Magnus, that's obvious to anyone with eyes, but she doesn't love Doyle's Grange." She lifted her head, and Crispin used the side of his thumb to wipe away her tears. "I knew there was no hope when she didn't laugh after Magnus told her his ridiculous joke about how it came to be called Doyle's Grange."

"She didn't?"

"No. And that's why I have to marry Jeremy." She gripped the lapels of his coat. "I can't stay here. I can't. I'm not a good enough person for that. I'll go mad if I stay, and if I don't go mad, then one day I'll say something to her I shouldn't, and Magnus must take her side."

Crispin stroked a hand over her head. "But him?" He spoke in a low voice. "The man's not worthy of you."

"You don't know that." She pushed away from him. "I shouldn't have said anything."

He followed her to the very rear of the lawn but needed another step to come even. They were off the path, both of them moving quickly.

She spoke before he'd caught up. "Magnus likes him."

"Magnus tolerates him because he thinks you love the man."

She put out a hand to slow him down. "Oh, do watch where you put your feet. You'll step—"

"What?"

She stopped walking. But Crispin, being a tall man and in the middle of a step, moved those few inches more. She cried out. Too late. His foot came down on the grass. "Look what you've done."

"What? What have I done?" He followed her downward glance with a puzzled expression.

"You've killed it." Tears burned in her eyes and choked off her words until she managed to swallow. "There's little enough beauty here anymore. Eleanor is determined to ruin it all, and now you're destroying what's left for me to enjoy. There's nothing else here I love. Not anymore."

"I'm sorry." It was plain he'd no idea what he'd done. None at all.

"You're not." She stared at the crocus that he'd smashed into the dirt, and all she could see was her future if she stayed. She knelt by the flattened plant.

"You're not sorry at all. Don't pretend you are. This one's managed to escape her, and now you've crushed it, and it's dead."

Crispin crouched across from her and pushed away her hand. He built up a wall of mud and propped the flower on it. "There. Perhaps like the rowan it will recover with some benign neglect."

"It won't." Those were tears thickening her voice, but she met his gaze head on. "If it survives the day, Eleanor will find it, and she'll tell Hob to dig it up. If she doesn't kill it with her own bare hands. That's all she ever does: murder what I love and all the time she makes it impossible to be angry at her."

He frowned at the mud on his gloves. With a hard sigh, he pulled them off and dropped them in his coat pocket. Then, both of them still bent over the plant, he tapped the underside of her chin. "I'm sorry I was clumsy and trod on your flower. I'm sorry Eleanor digs them up." He took her hand and brought her to her feet. "I'm an oaf. I don't watch where I put my feet. And now I've made you unhappy when that's the last thing I meant to do. Listen to me." He grabbed her by the shoulders again, and she looked at him through a blur of tears. "I'll have the groundskeeper plant a hundred of them at Wordless. You can go there every day to see them. She won't be able to ruin them for you there."

Her chest was stuffed full of feelings, and she could not contain them all. "A hundred isn't enough."

"A thousand then." With her hand still in his, he walked them toward the rear of the house.

"It's too late for that, Crispin. I'll soon be living too far away to walk to Wordless."

His mouth thinned. "Then you can bloody well live at Wordless. I don't mind if you do. I'm never there. Why oughtn't you?"

"Because then everyone will think I'm your lover, that's why."

"It wouldn't be true."

Emptiness settled in her belly and made everything familiar and dear seem unfamiliar, from Doyle's Grange to Crispin to her future life. "You've not changed a bit, have you? Still full of grand and impossible ideas. I might as well make my home in the clouds as live at Wordless."

He cupped her face and brushed his thumbs across her cheeks, and when he did that and looked at her the way he was now, the world with all its troubles dropped away. When he touched her like that, she believed she could live in a castle in the sky.

"Do you feel that?" he whispered. "Whenever I touch you there's nothing but that heat."

"I cannot live on that."

"He's not your equal."

She blinked several times, but the heat coursing through her stayed. "Of course he is."

"He's not." He dipped his head and for a breathless moment she thought he meant to kiss her. She could no more deny the passion between them than she could deny herself air. He moved his finger again. "You're cold."

She drew her head back, and his finger slipped away. "Your hands are warm."

"You've made up your mind, haven't you?"

She nodded.

"Nothing will shake your conviction that he's more than he is?"

"He's what I need him to be."

He shook his head. "Don't. It's a mistake. Don't marry just to get away. I, of all people, know what a mistake that is."

She swallowed hard. "I can't stay here. I can't."

"Not even if it's good sense? You're running from a bad situation into a worse one, and it's one you can't take back when the hard light of reason proves your mistake." He kept his voice low. "I promise you, there's nothing worse than to marry where there is no love."

"She's ruined Doyle's Grange for me. Ruined it."

"He's a belly on him and only half a head of hair. No doubt he's losing his hearing." He checked himself and after a glance at the house, lowered his voice. "Do you want to spend the best years of your life shouting at a fat old man who probably never read a novel in his life? And if he did, he'd not think it grand."

While they stood here, the clouds had got thicker and darker and the air colder. She grasped his hand and pressed it. "He likes me, with my red hair and despite all my faults."

"Is he marrying a wife or a nurse for his mother?"

"That's uncalled for."

"It's entirely called for."

She recognized that mulish look. "You've never had to do without something you want, let alone something you need."

His eyes widened. "The hell I haven't."

"You? With ten thousand a month and houses all over England? He is a decent man. We understand one another."

"Don't attempt to tell me you love that man. I know what you look like when you're in love."

"It won't be the way you and I were." Her heart cracked open, irreparably broken, and there was just no way to repair the damage she'd done. "Not that kind of love, but then Jeremy and I are not young and foolish or in love for the first time. I daresay we'll get on quite well. I know we shall." She walked away from him. The chickens had been let out, and a few of the hens scattered as she and Crispin approached the back gate. "Besides," she said when he was next to her again, "he's no objection to me, not even at my advanced age."

His face emptied of emotion. "Marry me instead."

"You don't want that."

She knew from experience that Crispin, when angry, turned quiet. His gaze was quite capable of freezing one to death with a glance. No doubt he'd learned that from his father. He went silent long enough to tie her stomach in knots. She waited him out and won that contest, for he spoke in a low, tight, voice. "Have you more to say about how I think or feel?"

"You'll always resent me for what happened, for the choice I made. You were steadfast, and I was not."

"I don't blame you. Not for what my father did to you. To us."

"You haven't forgiven me."

"You willfully misunderstand." He touched her arm, and she flinched. "It's not I who hasn't forgiven. It's you."

Her mouth gaped. "I do not blame you. Not for your father, that's hardly your fault, and not for anything else."

"You can't forgive yourself."

She drew in a stuttering breath. "What sort of person would I be if I did?"

"The woman I used to love."

"I'm not that woman. Don't you see? There's no repairing what happened. I'm broken. Nothing will ever fix that."

Chapter Twelve

The following day

NORTHWORD LEANED FORWARD on the chair he'd brought next to Magnus's and breathed in the scent of the beer that filled his mug. They were in Magnus's office, sitting on chairs drawn up to the fireplace. It was just after one, and the remains of their luncheon were on the table by the door. That arse-kissing toady Jeremy Stewart had driven his mother, Eleanor, and Portia to Aubry Sock for tea. They weren't expected back for another three hours at least. That left him and Magnus with the house to themselves. They were taking full advantage.

He reached behind him and flipped open the box of cigars on the table. He gave Magnus cigars whenever they saw each other. Northword fished out two and handed one over before he hefted his mug. "Good friends and happy marriages." He did not intend for his toast to extend to Portia and that prick Jeremy Stewart, so when Magnus raised his glass he narrowed the scope of his words. "To you and Eleanor."

While the April sky might be blue, it was bloody cold outside. The nearest window was open a crack to let out the smoke. The office where they sat was on the small side of cozy, with shelves jammed with books, a desk with stacks of pamphlets, papers, a two-day-old *Times*, and a Bible. A trunk with broken trim sat underneath the window. An oak highboy painted red took up half the wall across from the fireplace. The table behind them, close enough for them to use it, was covered with paper. Magnus's doing, that riot of thick, odd-sized sheets of paper.

Charcoal and gum rubber littered the surface, and Crispin had flicked away a pencil that rolled underneath the cigar box. Several of the pages were sketches of the view from various windows of the house or of everyday items: a cup, an apple, a Bible seen from the page edges. Some were of furniture, a view of a window, and more recently, the church in Aubry Sock where Magnus, naturally, had spent a great deal of time before he had the living in West Aubry. There were a few sketches of him and several of the men and women who lived near Up Aubry. He had a knack for taking a likeness.

Magnus lifted his mug, recently filled from the contents of the earthenware jug he'd brought back from Up Aubry earlier in the day. The tavern there was half the size of this room and comfortably held the entire male population of the village, counting the proprietor and including Crispin. They served a dark and bitter beer that had to be the finest anywhere in England. "To good friends." He winked. He took a long draw on his beer, and when he was done, let out a sigh. "Light the bloody thing."

"Impatient sod." He leaned over with a candle for Magnus to use to light his cigar. He lit his when Magnus blew the first puff of smoke in the direction of the open window.

"If the subject should happen to come up, don't mention the cigars to Eleanor."

"Why not?"

Magnus contorted in order to tap the top of the cigar box. "She'll have my head if she finds out about these. Thinks smoking is vile. Ungodly for a man of God."

Crispin didn't reply right away "Are you telling me you aren't permitted to smoke a fine cigar in your own house?"

"Not just my house now." He let out a stream of smoke. "There's always the vicarage in West Aubry, but it's smaller than here. Lovely, make no mistake, but she's taken a fancy to the Grange, Eleanor has. It's here she wants to live."

"If she complains, tell her it was me, and that you tried to dissuade me." He drew on his cigar. When he'd let out the smoke, he said, "Tell her I said I am the bloody Viscount Northword, and I can smoke a cigar anywhere I damn please."

Magnus laughed. "Perhaps I'll not say precisely that. But she'll agree with the sentiment, I tell you that."

"Tell her I refused to save my soul, but that yours remains unsullied."

"That I will." They sat for a bit, contemplating the fire and the warmth and the hint of chill at their backs. "Did Lady Northword mind you smoking?"

"Never. Though to be fair, I never did around her. The way you won't around your wife." He tried for a smoke ring and muffed it. "I don't think less of you for that."

"Your bloody house is big enough you could have a dozen men smoking and no one at the other end would know." Magnus exhaled then sank a little lower on his chair. "Put another bit of coal on the fire, won't you?"

"Why should I when you're nearer?"

"Because I'm more comfortable than you. Because I'm an old married man now. I need my strength." He put his finger in the stream of smoke leaving his mouth and traced it upward as far as his arm could reach. When he'd settled again on his chair, he examined his cigar. "The last cigar to be smoked at the Grange. What would Doyle say if he were still alive?"

"Arf. Arf."

Magnus's belly shook. "The poor dog froze to death, I hear. For lack of coal on the fire."

"God help us all if the Grange must be renamed 'Doyle and Magnus's Grange.'"

"I'll carve it on my headstone. 'Doyle was a fine dog, but Magnus was the better man.'"

"Amen, my friend. Amen." They laughed at that together, and when Crispin was back on his chair, having added half a scuttle of coal to the fire, they smoked in companionable silence. He stretched his legs as close to the grate as he dared. The wind rattled the shutters harder, then died away. "Will it rain soon, do you think?"

Magnus nodded. "They'll be home early, I expect, Portia and Eleanor and the others. Oh damn." He shot to his feet, wiping at his waistcoat.

"Have you burnt it?" Crispin asked.

"Devil take me if I have. I think so."

"It's good you're a married man." He laughed. "You need looking after."

"So do you." Magnus stared at the spot where hot cigar ash had eaten a hole in the fabric. "Eleanor will have my head." He brushed at his waistcoat before he sat again. "Portia will mend it for me, and not tell Eleanor, either. Solid as a rock, that girl. But then you know that."

"I do."

After several minutes more silence, Crispin put down his cigar and reached for a stack of the papers on the table. He went through them slowly, with the reverence due the pages. As always, he was in awe of Magnus's talent. His art. Magnus Temple was a bloody genius, and here he was, the vicar of West Aubry when he ought to be in London painting for the Royal Academy. What a waste. What a bloody crime. Portia blamed herself for that, when really the blame belonged to his father. And to him. For not foreseeing that his father would threaten not Portia directly but the people she loved. "Why are all these out?"

"Organizing things." Magnus shrugged. "Clearing out the old now that Eleanor's here. I try to do some every few days."

There were several drawings of Eleanor, including one in which she was clearly the inspiration for a Madonna. Crispin came to a portrait of Portia, done a few years ago. So young. His heart hurt to see her. She'd never been a conventional beauty, but he doubted any man would deny her appeal. Spend five minutes with her, and you'd soon be convinced you'd never met a finer woman. In the portrait, done in pen and ink, her head was bowed in concentration. Magnus had drawn just the tops of her hands, enough to show she held a needle. Behind her was the suggestion of the parlor fireplace. One expected she might at any moment lift her head and smile. A wave of lust hit him, pulling him under. He laid the stack of sketches on his lap, the portrait of Portia on top.

She still thought about the baby they'd made, when all these years he'd convinced himself she didn't. How could he blame her for what she'd done as a sixteen year old girl in a desperate situation? His father had all but guaranteed she would carry that burden alone. There were women in her situation who died, and that knowledge chilled him to the marrow. She might have died, and a world without her would have been a barren place.

"My wife's been gone more than a year, now. Nearly two."

"We were sorry to hear that news, Portia and I."

"I was a better man after I was married." Marriage had agreed with him, that was true. Not a perfect union, but not a bad one either. He'd been happy in a calmer way. His wife had been a fine and admirable woman, and he had always hated himself for not loving her as she deserved.

"You'll marry again." Magnus nodded to himself. "You must. Unnatural if you don't."

"That's so." He did not have a son yet, and that must be remedied.

"Have you met anyone who will do?"

He shook his head, but Jesus, the lie of his denial spread ashes across his soul.

"Pity."

"I don't like Stewart."

Magnus took another pull of his beer. "He writes verses. Did he tell you that? No? I expect that's why Portia's set herself on marrying him. The poetry did her in, that's what I think. Lord knows she's never paid any attention to other man, and they've come calling. I know you don't see her like that, but there's a good many men who've wanted to marry her."

He did not move for fear of Magnus seeing more than he ought, but then he wondered if that wasn't a worse way to lie to his best friend than if he plastered on a disbelieving grin. "Is that so?"

"He's not bad, you know. Stewart."

Crispin snorted.

"As a poet." Magnus slunk lower on his chair. "Goes on about cliffs and bluebells flashing with dew. But there's one about a stag I like. Noble antlers and beams of sunrise."

"He's an architect, I thought."

Magnus reached over and tapped the underside of the sketches on Crispin's lap hard enough to make the paper jump. "Only one of his occupations puts money in his pocket."

He slumped on his chair. A poet? The man was a damned poet? "God save us from poets."

"The Lord will strike you dead for that." Magnus grinned and the lines of his face deepened, and it seemed to Crispin there were more now than there had been the last time he'd seen Magnus. "Might take fifty years, though."

He picked up Magnus's portrait of Portia, and something tugged at him as he studied the smiling woman on the page. She was unhappy now, and she did not deserve to be. Not then, and not now. He glanced at Magnus.

The words that came to his lips felt odd and foreign and right. They shook loose from wherever they'd been lodged and flew into the air. "I want to marry Portia."

Magnus choked on his laughter.

He waited until there was silence again and then said, "I shall marry Portia."

A furrow appeared in Magnus's forehead. "You mean that."

"With your permission. Of course." He wanted this. He did. No more deception.

Magnus looked at him with his artist's eye, seeing what was there. And what was not. "What makes you say a thing like that?"

He worked through what Magnus had said and the careful way he'd said it and he felt as sick at heart and just as defiant as he had been when he'd said the words to his father. "You won't agree to my marrying her?"

"You're like a brother to me. You know that."

He pushed out of his slouch. He was. . . affronted. Magnus owed him this. He bloody owed Portia the life she ought to have had. "I feel the same. But that doesn't make Portia my sister."

All trace of Magnus's usual good humor vanished. He leaned forward and set his cigar against the ashtray. "No one could ask for a better friend than you."

He sat up the rest of the way. Magnus was telling him no? The insult pricked him. Dented his pride. More, though, it scared the hell out of him. "Why not?"

"Is it wise?"

"Yes, damn it, it is. Why wouldn't it be?"

Magnus shook his head.

The urge to spear him with a look of blue-blooded incredulity was impossible to resist. "I'd be a better husband to her than that doughty old poet she's going to marry so you and Eleanor can make a life together."

Magnus's eyebrows shot up. "Is that what she told you?"

"Not in so many words, but it's true. If she marries me, she'll want for nothing, you know that. I should think you'd be pushing her my way. Most brothers with unmarried sisters do."

It was Magnus's turn to be insulted. "I'd never. You know that."

"Yes. I do know that. Maybe you should have."

"You and Portia?"

"Why not? Why the bloody hell not, I should like to know?"

"If she'll have you." He rested a hand on Crispin's shoulder. "If she'll have you, you'd have my blessing."

"If she'll have me?" The bottom dropped from his stomach. If Magnus didn't think Portia would marry him, maybe she wouldn't. Maybe he'd never change her mind. "Why do you think she wouldn't if I asked her?"

"I shouldn't say this, but I think she used to be in love with you. After you left, the joy went out of her." He chewed on his lower lip. "I've watched her here, the two of you, and to be honest, whatever there was between you, one-sided as it was, it's long dead. I don't think you're what she needs. Not any more."

Chapter Thirteen

Four days later

HE DIDN'T LIKE the silence at all. In all the times he'd been at Doyle's Grange, the house had never been this quiet, not when Portia was here. Jesus, what if he was too late? What if while he'd been giving her time, Portia had convinced that ridiculous poet to take her to Gretna Green?

Hob came into the entryway and bowed his head. He wasn't wearing his livery. "Milord." He straightened. "Didn't expect to see thee here."

Out of pure habit, he took off his hat, but rather than hand it over to Hob, he hung it from one of the pegs above the doorway that led to the servant's quarters. "Where is everyone?"

"Gone. Or out."

"I see. Who is out and who is gone?"

"Mr. Stewart. Mrs. Stewart. They've gone."

"And Portia?"

"Out."

"With the Stewarts?"

"With the tree."

"Thank you. I'll just go see her then. I'll announce myself."

"Milord."

He left his hat on the peg and walked outside to the back of the house. She was sitting on the ground by the rowan tree, industriously doing something to the earth around the trunk. Her hands stilled when he had yet another five paces to cover.

"She'll dig them up next spring, but I don't care." With both hands, she tamped down the dirt around the rowan sapling. "I've planted a hundred of them here, and next spring they'll come up, and I'll be the only one who knows it's my name they're saying."

"The crocuses?"

She swiped a hand across her forehead and twisted a bit to look at him. There was a smear of dirt just at the part of her hair. "Yes. Why are you here?"

"Where is Mr. Stewart?"

Her hands fell to her lap. "I sent him away."

"Did you?" He held out his hand, and she put her gloved hand in his and stood.

She glanced away, then back. "He's a decent man, but you're right. He doesn't deserve a wife who will never love him."

He pulled her close and brushed the backs of his fingers across her cheek. "Don't be unhappy. You know I can't bear it."

His bare hand against her warm skin, a touch so light he hardly felt it, except he did. He remembered his mouth over hers and the dizzying wonder of finding her in his embrace again. This contact plunged through his body in the same way. He continued downward, caressing along her jaw, her throat. "I've done nothing but think about you since I left. Every second since I arrived. Before Wordless. After Wordless."

"I as well."

"Every bloody moment of the last ten years and, God willing, every moment of the rest of my life." He brought out his handkerchief and cleaned away the dirt on her forehead.

"Thank you."

"You're welcome." He removed her thick gardening gloves one at a time, and shoved them into his coat pocket. "Please. Hear me out. You're right, too. All along you've been right. We can't change the past, but we don't need to. Everything we need to know about each other we discovered that day at Wordless. If you don't believe me, I'll prove it to you again."

"Prove what?"

"That we are still in love. Despite what happened. Because of what happened. Will you let me show you?"

She tugged on her hand, and he tightened his fingers. "Here?"

"In private, if you don't mind." Her hand clasped in his, he dashed across the lawn to the back door. Inside, they caught their breath, and then headed upstairs, an urgent journey to his room.

Northword closed the door to his room as softly as he could. His fingers were tight around Portia's hand, and he didn't let go even after he turned the key in the lock. Arm straight down, he interlaced his fingers with hers. The palm of his other hand slapped on the wall above her shoulder, taking his weight while he leaned in and kissed her.

Eventually, they left off the frantic kissing and set themselves to an equally frantic removal of each other's clothes. It took some time to remove the layers, to untie knots and unfasten buttons. But they were still young and healthy and far, far wiser about such things than they'd once been.

When she stood in just her shift, he touched her gently, from cheek, to throat, to her collarbone. Her breath hitched when his fingers reached the top swell of her breast. "You see?" he murmured. "That's not changed. The way I react to you. Or you to me."

His palm dropped down, too, touching her breast, curving over her, and with that, the world narrowed to him and Portia and that was precisely right. He allowed himself a smug smile. Again, he brushed just the tip of his finger over her. "Is that good?"

"Yes. Damn you, yes."

"Think how it would feel if you were naked." God, he loved to see her face when she was in passion.

"Beast."

Her name was a sigh on his breath. He kissed her, one hand cupping the back of her neck, the other fully curved over her breast, molding her there so that he could push her breast higher. His tongue flicked out and followed the seam of her lips, and she opened her mouth and for him, it was like falling under her spell all over again.

He pulled away and cupped her face in his hands. She wrapped her fingers around his wrists, but that was all. They stayed like that, touching each other, settling into the familiarity of the contact and this time, there was a sense of the world coming right.

His torso pressed against her as he leaned him and kissed her ear. "I love you, Portia Temple."

He wanted her now and afterward, and that was that. He wanted her in his life, this amazingly lovely creature who kissed with such delicate fever. Portia, who had inhabited his dreams for a decade. Portia, who had become a woman he admired and respected. He drew back before he completely lost control.

"How can you?"

"Because you are brave and strong and when I am with you, I want to see you laugh and smile. Because you would never, ever, ever put milk in my tea and tell me it's good for my health."

She gasped, and her fingers tightened around him. "She makes Magnus drink it that way, too." They laughed together at that and then she draped an arm around the back of his neck, and set the other around his naked waist, fingers angled downward. "She did the same to me once, but I poured it all in the slop bowl. She nearly came to tears. Poor Magnus."

"Poor me. You're not naked yet." He let go of her hand and fumbled at her shift while he kissed her, open mouthed, tongue involved. She kissed him back because Portia never did anything halfway. Her shift dropped to the floor with the rest of their clothes.

If Satan himself demanded his soul for this, he'd gladly hand it over.

"I want you in my arms. I want us skin to skin. I want to make you spend and call on God and me. I want your mouth on me, your hands, your thighs around me. I want your eyes glazed with passion for me." He took a step toward her. "I want to hear us both groan when I am inside you."

Northword leaned against her, his cock hard and him halfway to coming because, God save him, Portia's body was soft and curved, and he was going to make love to her until they were witless fools, and she had no choice but to agree they belonged together. She pushed up to kiss him again, and she was so very, very good at setting fire to his blood.

Lust, an unfathomable need, came from deep inside him, and it was everything he'd missed every damned time he'd had sexual relations. It wasn't that he hadn't loved his wife. He had. Or that he hadn't enjoyed other lovers who came to his bed. He had. But not like this. Never. The missing part of his soul clicked into place with her, and he was whole as he had not been since the day his father had engineered their split.

Every shiver of her body, every soft sound to fall on his ears mattered to him because this was Portia in his arms. Failing to please her would rip him to pieces. He pushed away from her and grabbed her hand while he walked backward to the bed, bringing her along. No half measures. No caution.

Portia laughed and gave him a push. The backs of his legs hit the bed, and he sat on the mattress, splayed out to catch his balance. She stepped between his spread legs, and he touched her naked backside or just stared at her breasts.

He drew her to him, hands sliding along her waist, up her back, fingers dancing down the dip of her spine. He took her mouth, and she answered with a taking of her own. He cupped her bottom and brought her up until she had her knees on the mattress on either side of his hips. She gripped the top of his shoulders until she had her balance and when she did he pulled the pins from her hair and kept going until her hair, dark, dark red, curled around his fingers.

"I adore your hair, every curl."

"I'm glad you like brunettes."

"My darling, you are deluded." He took some of her hair in his hand. Light from the window nearest her reflected off her hair, turning even the shadows a rich, dark red. "Your hair is red, and I adore every lock on your head." He slid his fingers beneath her chin and brought her face back to his. "I want you again. I want inside you now." He leaned forward and nipped her lower lip. "Anything you want, if you'll let me do that."

Her smile was everything he loved about Portia. Her smile was bright and bold and for him, and her smile had been living inside him for years. A part of Crispin Hope and a part of the man who had become the Viscount Northword.

"Although I feel I ought to tell you that I am inclined to be selfish just now." For this slice of time, he was looking not at Portia, but solely at a naked woman whose proportions pleased him inordinately. Wickedly so. He brushed her hair behind her shoulders. In ten years, she'd become a woman. "You're still beautiful, more beautiful and desirable than ever." He put his palm over her mound, slid a finger between, and found slick heat. "That's lovely." He drew in a breath. "You're wet for me."

"Yes."

"Good, because I'm hard for you." Jesus, he wanted those legs around him. He wanted his hips tucked up tight against hers. He swept the back of his hand across her shoulder then down to her breast. "Lovely. That's a fact."

Her nipples peaked, and he swept his fingers across her again. His belly hollowed out. Somewhere in the house, timbers creaked. Outside, rain pattered against the windows. Then harder until it beat on the roof and windows. He held his breath until he was sure the noise was just settlement and the rain and they weren't about to be interrupted by a furious Hob.

He leaned close, his mouth by her ear. "What I'd like to do isn't decent at all. It's wicked and depraved."

She angled her body against his. "You make it sound delicious. Is it?"

He fit both his hands over her breasts, and she leaned into his palms. He looked his fill of the sight, his hands over her, the flesh he couldn't cover, the way her mouth parted. He pressed his lips to her shoulder: a light kiss while he swept his fingers along the underside of her breast, one then the other, and the curve of her devastated him. He brushed a finger over her nipple and saw, felt and reacted to the way she hardened at his touch. "I want my mouth here." His fingertip came to rest at her mons then slid down until his hand cupped her. "And here."

Her eyes opened wide, and she tipped her head to one side, curious. Intrigued. "There?"

"Yes. Precisely there."

She arranged herself on his bed, her hair spread out, and her body open for him. He joined her and slid his hands underneath her bottom. One thing he'd learned was that he loved the taste of a woman. He'd had a mistress before he married, a courtesan who taught him things he hadn't worked out on his own with Portia or some other woman who could never measure up.

Portia gave herself over to his mouth on her, and he made damned sure he didn't bring her too fast. He adored her moans, the tension in her body when she came close, the way her hands touched his head, the tilt of her pelvis toward him. She made him feel like the best lover in the world, and the proof was in the way she came.

For a fraction of time, she went completely still, and in that space he spread her nether lips and licked along the center of her sex. She came apart, holding back none of her pleasure.

"More, Crispin." Her voice shook. "More."

He pulled himself over her, his mouth by her ear. "You have all of me. There's nothing more for me to give." He touched her once, and she flinched with unsatisfied passion. "You have everything."

He moved down her body and before long she devolved into an incoherent cry. He spread his fingers over her belly while she came back to earth and then pulled himself up enough to dip his tongue into her navel. He lifted his head, and when she was looking at him, soft-eyed with pleasure, he thought his heart would burst as past and present emotions warred in him. As they did in her, too.

Northword spread his fingers over her stomach again. He had to work to keep his voice steady and then decided the battle wasn't worth fighting. "Portia." Her name came in a whisper. "I wanted you to have my child. I still do. I want it enough to beg you for another chance. We were young. You're right about that. But I wanted us. And our child."

"I know. I know. I know."

"Say you'll marry me, Portia. Promise it." He stared at her stomach, fingers sliding, but tipped his head so he could see her face, too. Eyes closed, lips edged with white. "We can have the child we make tonight. Marry me. Please. I'm a better man, a wiser man. I'd be a proper husband to you and a loving father. Magnus knows I want to marry you. He doesn't think you will, but I don't give a damn for his opinion."

"Crispin."

He took her hand and moved over her, one leg across hers. The slide of his skin over hers heated his blood, the very marrow of him, and he pushed her shoulder until she was on her back. She opened herself to him. He pulled himself over her and thrust inside.

She was hot and slick, and he got harder being inside her—and inside, her soft body barely gave. He put his forearms above her shoulders and kept still, giving her time to adjust to him. "I couldn't bear the thought of that man touching you." He drew back his hips and pushed forward. "Nor the thought of you touching him. Nor that you might fall in love with him."

She put her hands on either side of his face and arched her pelvis toward him. "Hush, my love."

He drew back and pushed slowly in again, and it was heaven. Tension sang between them and for him it was the certainty that he could do exactly what he wanted, what would please then both, and the fact of her woman's body that sent him into sensual paradise. He stroked in her steadily, and before long he knew he wouldn't last much longer.

He stopped moving, and that nearly killed him, holding back all the urges of his body. He took her head between his hands, weight on his forearms. "Marry me." He drew back his hips and pushed forward enough to make his balls go tight. He stopped moving because otherwise he couldn't think. He had to work to marshal his thoughts.

"Marry me because I love you. Marry me because you love me. We'll have children. Us. God, Portia, please. I want what slipped away before. I don't want to live without you. I love you. I've always loved you."

With the last of his wits, the last bit of his coherence, he waited.

She put her hands on either side of his face. "I love you, too, Crispin Hope. I always have."

"Marry me."

She wrapped her legs around his hips and bit his ear lobe once. "Yes, you fool. Yes. Now do this properly. The way you promised me, or I shall know you'll never be a proper husband for me."

And so he did.

About Carolyn Jewel

Carolyn Jewel was born on a moonless night. That darkness was seared into her soul and she became an award-winning and USA Today bestselling author of historical and paranormal romance. She has a very dusty car and a Master's degree in English that proves useful at the oddest times. An avid fan of fine chocolate, finer heroines, Bollywood films, and heroism in all forms, she has two cats and two dogs. Also a son. One of the cats is his.

Visit Carolyn on the web at:

carolynjewel.com

Twitter: @cjewel

Facebook: facebook.com/carolynjewelauthor

Goodreads: goodreads.com/cjewel

Sign up for Carolyn's **newsletter** (http://cjewel.me/newsletter15) so you never miss a new book and get exclusive, subscriber-only content.

Excerpts

A NOTORIOUS RUIN
CHAPTER 1

London, 1818

CYNSSYR GLARED AT the door to number twenty-four Portman Square. "Blast it," he said to the groom who held two other horses. "What the devil is taking them so long?" He sat his horse with authority, a man in command of himself and his world. His buckskins fit close over lean thighs, and the exacting cut of his jacket declared a tailor of some talent. A Pink of the Ton, he seemed, but for eyes that observed more than they revealed.

"The Baron's a family man now, sir." The groom stamped his feet and tucked his hands under his armpits.

"What has that to do with anything?"

A handbill abandoned by some reveler from one of last night's fetes skimmed over the cobbles and spooked the other two horses, a charcoal gelding by the name of Poor Boy on account of the loss of his equine manhood; and a muscular dun. The groom had a dicey moment what with the cold having numbed his fingers but managed to send the sheet skittering to freedom.

"Man with a family can't leave anywhere spot on the dot," the groom said.

"I don't see why."

The door to number twenty-four flew open with a ringing crack of wood against stone. Of the two men who came out, the taller was Benjamin Dunbartin, Baron Aldreth, the owner of the house. He moved down the stairs at a rapid clip, clapping his hat onto his blond head as if he meant to cement it in place. The other man gripped his hat in one hand and descended at a more leisurely pace. The wind whipped a mass of inky curls over his sharp cheekbones.

"My lord." The groom handed Benjamin the reins to the dun. Before the groom could so much as offer a leg up, Ben launched himself into the saddle without a word of greeting or acknowledgment. Most everyone liked Benjamin. With his good looks and boyish smile, it was practically impossible not to. At the moment, however, Cynssyr thought Ben did not look like a man who cared for the family life.

"Come along, Devon," Benjamin said to his companion. He spoke with such force his dun tossed its head and pranced in nearly a full circle before Ben had him under control again.

Cynssyr's green eyes widened. "Have you quarreled with Mary?"

"Certainly not," said Ben.

"Well, you look like you've been hit by lightning from on high and still hear the angels singing. What's put you in such a state?"

"None of your damned business." The dun stamped hard on the cobbles, and Ben swore under his breath.

Cynssyr's bay snorted, and he reached to soothe the animal. "I should say it is, if I'm to endure such behavior from you."

"Devon!"

"Is this, by any chance, about Devon's letter?"

Ben's neck fairly snapped, he turned so quickly. "What do you know about that damned letter?"

"He wouldn't let me read it, but it must have succeeded. Camilla Fairchild is too young to be looking at a man that way." Cynssyr's mouth quirked and with the slight smile his austere features softened. When he smiled, he was about as handsome as a man could get, a fact not lost on him. He knew quite well the effect of his smile on the fairer sex.

Devon reached the curb in time to overhear the last remark. Coal-black eyes, at the moment completely without humor, slid from Ben to Cynssyr. "Disgraceful, ain't it? Her mother ought to set the girl a better example." He, too, accepted the reins of his gelding from the groom. He glanced at the stairs.

"Do you think she will?" Cynssyr managed, quite deliberately, to sound as though he hoped she wouldn't. Christ, he hoped not. He fully expected to soon discover what Mrs. Fairchild's backside felt like under his hands. Soft, he imagined. Energetic, he hoped.

"You ought to know better, Cyn," Devon said. "Even Mary said so."

"You will be relieved to know that at lord Sather's rout Miss Fairchild's passion was as yet untempered by experience. I merely provided her some." His smile reappeared. "A regrettably small amount, to be sure."

"You know, Cyn," Ben said, "one of these days you're going to miscalculate and find yourself married to some featherbrained female who'll bore you to tears."

"What else have you done, Devon, that's made him such wretched company?" Cynssyr kept one eye on Benjamin.

"Not one word," Ben said, glaring not at Cynssyr but at Devon.

Devon stopped with one foot in the stirrup to gift the world with affronted innocence. "All I did was—"

"Not one!" Ben turned a warning glance on him, too. "Not a word from you, either, Cyn."

Dev shook his head and mounted, exchanging a glance with Cynssyr who shrugged and found himself still mystified.

Only when the three were long out of earshot of the groom and riding toward Hyde Park did Ben speak. "How dare you?" He took a crumpled sheet of paper from his pocket and thrust it at Devon. "How dare you!"

"My personal correspondence is none of your affair." Devon, who had never expected to come into his title, could nevertheless exude more condescension than ever his father had managed, and the previous earl had been a master.

"Give me one reason I oughtn't call you out."

"Now see here," Cynssyr said, more than a little alarmed.

"Frankly, Cyn, if you knew about the letter, I ought to have satisfaction from you, too." Ben turned back to Devon. "Well?"

"I asked permission to court her when we were at Rosefeld for your wedding. But I had not the proper credentials then." Devon laughed bleakly. "I am Bracebridge now."

"Four years ago," Cynssyr said, "Camilla Fairchild was all of what, twelve or thirteen?"

"Good God," said Benjamin. "Not Miss Fairchild."

Devon snatched the crumpled paper from Ben's hand. "I won't lose her a second time."

"Lose whom?" Cynssyr drew even with Devon. "What are you two talking about? Devon, I thought your letter was for Miss Fairchild." Two women out for a morning walk stopped their stroll to stare at the men riding by. Out of pure habit, Cynssyr gave them an assessing glance, which made Devon laugh.

"Have you declared yourself?" Ben waved at the paper in Devon's hand. "Besides in that note of yours, I mean."

"If not Miss Fairchild, then whom?" Cynssyr said, by now more than a little annoyed. "Miss George?" When that got no reply, he said, "Not Miss Willowby. Oh, please, no. If it's Miss Willowby, I forbid it."

Devon slid the note into his pocket. "She has not the slightest idea of my feelings."

"Good God."

"Now that she is here in London," Devon said, "I mean to change that." He pulled back on his black, waiting for Ben's dun to draw alongside. Once again, Cynssyr found himself maddeningly excluded. "With your permission, of course."

"It isn't my permission you need be concerned with," Ben said. "It's her father's."

"The old man can bugger himself for all I care." The black-as-the-depths-of-hell eyes that even Cynssyr, who knew better, sometimes thought devoid of life flashed with a violent fire.

Benjamin grinned.

They were at the Park now, off the streets and onto the riding paths. "Would one of you," said Cynssyr, "please tell me what the devil you're talking about?"

"Dev thinks he's in love."

"That much I gathered." He looked over at Devon. "In love with whom?"

"My sister-in-law," Ben said, throwing up one hand. "That's who."

Cynssyr gave Devon a look. "Which one?" He moved out of the path of a fat gentleman on a white mare. To the best of his recollection, there were four Sinclair sisters and Benjamin had married one of them. That left three. And, if memory served, the Sinclair sisters deserved their reputation for beauty. Ben's wife, Mary, was among the most beautiful women of Cynssyr's rather vast acquaintance. He almost didn't blame Ben for marrying her.

"I don't *think* I'm in love."

"The youngest? Miss Emily?" His green eyes flickered with interest. "If she turns out half as beautiful as she promised, she'll cause a riot at her debut."

"No. And stay the hell away from Emily, Cyn."

"Then it must be the brunette. Lucy." The name rolled off his tongue replete with his recollection of ebony hair and features of heartbreaking perfection.

"No."

"You mean the eldest?" He could not for the life of him summon an image of the eldest Sinclair sister. "That's impossible. I don't even remember her."

"Blonde? Gray-blue eyes. Yay tall." Ben indicated an inch or so below his chin which meant a tall woman, perhaps even an ungainly one. "You'll meet her tonight at the ball. Meet her again, that is."

"Why don't I recall her?" Cynssyr glanced at Devon.

"And by the way," Ben said. "Stay away from Lucy, too."

"Why?"

"Because when it comes to women, damn you, Cynssyr, you're a rogue, that's why."

"Mama begins to despair. Perhaps I ought put to rest her doubts of a succession."

Ben snorted. "I'd not curse any of my sisters-in-law with you for a husband."

"Now that," Cynssyr said, "wounds me deeply. When at last I marry, I expect I'll make a most excellent husband."

"Hah," said Devon.

"*Et tu, Brute?*"

"You can't even settle on what woman to seduce tonight."

"If not for Napoleon, I'd likely be years married. A positive dullard, like Ben here." But Napoleon there was, so Cynssyr wasn't married at all. Love, naturally, would have but a limited role in any marriage he contracted. The war had burned out his capacity, if ever he'd possessed it, for such saving emotion.

"A dullard?" said Ben, spoiling his attempt to appear insulted by breaking into laughter. Devon rolled his eyes.

"Whatever you two think, I'm quite aware I need a wife. A man of my station requires a wife, as my desperate mother so often reminds me."

"God help the woman fool enough to marry you," Ben said.

"Why not one of your sisters-in-law, Ben? It seems an excellent idea." Dozens of suitable candidates were thrown his way every season, this one being no different from any other since the war. But he'd not been able to bring himself to the sticking point with any of them.

"No."

"I'll reform." He grinned. "I promise."

"You'll reform when hell freezes over."

A faint memory tickled at the back of his mind. He tapped his temple. "You mean the spinster, don't you, Devon? The eldest. The one with the spectacles."

"Blond hair, gray-blue eyes. Yay tall," Benjamin repeated.

"What was her name?"

Ben's blue eyes chilled another degree. "Anne."

"Gad. I still don't remember her. Except for the spectacles." He looked askance at Dev. "I have never understood his taste in women."

"You truly want to marry Anne?" Ben asked Devon. Curiosity and relief lingered at the edges of the question, but hearing him, no one could doubt the seriousness of the matter. No doting father could have sounded more cautious.

"Yes."

"I meant to introduce her to Declan McHenry," said Ben, looking thoughtfully at Devon. "Or Phillip Lovejoy."

"I'd be obliged if you didn't."

"Good God, you are serious, aren't you?"

"It's been four years. I am done waiting." Amusement brightened Devon's brooding eyes and made his severe mouth curve in a surprisingly warm smile. It did interesting things to his face, the way severity gave way to warmth. At times like this, when he saw Devon smile, Cynssyr understood exactly why women went so eagerly to his bed.

If Devon had really decided the Sinclair spinster was the woman he wanted, then the matter was done. He would have his way. The why of it mystified him. Even as plain Devon Carlisle, he could do far better than some dried-up female who wasn't even pretty enough to bother taking off her spectacles. As matrimonial material, the earl of Bracebridge was nearly as sought after as he himself. Nearly. But, not quite.

"Enough. No more blather about love and marriage, you two," Cynssyr said. With a flick of the reins, he steered his horse past a fallen branch then cantered to the edge of a meadow where he waited for Ben and Devon.

"Jade," Ben accused when he reached the meadow.

Cynssyr flashed a brilliantly arrogant smile. "The trouble with you, my lord Baron Aldreth, is you love your wife. And you, Devon. For shame. You disappoint me. You disappoint all our sex, falling for this Miss Sinclair."

"Love," said Dev with one of his wry grins. "A most heinous crime."

"Love." Cynssyr lifted one brow in the supercilious disdain he usually reserved for certain rebuttals in the Lords. "You mean a man's delusion he's not been robbed of his freedom and a woman's that she's gained hers?"

"Exactly," Devon said.

"How can you trust your judgment now?" He lifted his riding whip, but brought it down on his boot leg, not his horse. "Fools the both of you." So saying, he urged his horse to a gallop. "Anne Sinclair," he muttered. He heard Devon and Ben thunder after him and gave his horse its head. They had no chance of catching him now. Only the best horseflesh found its way into his stables. He had the best of everything. Wine. Horses. Women. Friends.

He wanted to roar with disgust and dismay. Devon married. What was he to do with himself then? To the devil with spinsters who set their caps on marriage, he thought as the chill wind whipped past him. "To the very devil with her." Thus did the duke of Cynssyr, so deservedly referred to as Lord Ruin, dismiss the woman with whom he would soon be desperately in love.

INDISCREET
CHAPTER 1

LORD EDWARD MARRACK refused more wine when the bottle came around in his direction. Instead, he leaned against his chair while his friend the Earl of Crosshaven raised a hand—Cross was inevitably the center of attention—and said, with significant stress, the two words, "Sabine Godard."

The other men in the room looked impressed. No one, including Lord Edward, doubted for a moment that Cross had indeed secured the person of Miss Sabine Godard.

Up to now, the young lady's reputation had been unassailable. She was an orphan who had been raised by her uncle since she was quite young. They made their home in Oxford, the city of spires, Henry Godard having been a don there and a noted philosopher until his recent retirement from those hallowed walls. She and her uncle had come to London so that Godard could receive a knighthood in recognition of his intellectual contributions to king and empire.

They had not been long in London, the Godards, but Lord Edward recalled hearing Miss Godard was reckoned a pretty girl. Very pretty and quite unavailable. She was, if he had his facts in order, her uncle's permanent caretaker, as was often the fate of children not raised by their parents. Her uncle was now Sir Henry Godard. By several large steps, quite a come up in the world for them both.

The unavailable Miss Godard had been pursued by Crosshaven. That, too, Lord Edward had heard. The Earl of Crosshaven was angelically, devilishly, beautiful. His manners were exquisite and his intellect absolutely first-rate. Lord Edward would not bother with a friendship if that were not the case. But Crosshaven, in Lord Edward's opinion, was not as familiar with discretion as he might be. Something he was proving tonight.

Though Lord Edward liked Cross exceedingly, this boast of his was infamous. Ungentlemanly, in fact. That Cross had refilled his glass far too often in the course of the evening was no excuse for his revealing to anyone that he had seduced a young woman of decent family. And, one presumed, abandoned her to whatever fate her uncle might decide was fit for a girl who strayed from what was proper.

"How was she?" asked one of the other young bucks.

Cross kissed the tips of his fingers and arced his thus blessed hand toward the ceiling. That engendered several ribald comments, some having to do with Cross's prowess in the bedroom and others having to do with Sabine Godard and what Crosshaven may or may not have taught her about sexual congress and how to fornicate with élan.

In Lord Edward's opinion, Cross, though just short of thirty, and for all his lofty titles, had now proved he had a great deal to learn about honor and decency. This evening, which had begun as a pleasant interlude with men he liked, no longer seemed very pleasant.

"A seduction," Lord Edward said to no one in particular, "when properly carried out, pleases both parties for the duration, while a break humiliates no one."

"Who says I've broken with her?" Crosshaven asked.

"I do," he replied. "And any fool with half a brain."

Crosshaven shook his head sadly. "Is this what happens to a man when he falls in love? If I didn't know better, I'd accuse you of not wanting to go to bed with a pretty young woman." He winked. "Without benefit of marriage, I mean." He gave Lord Edward a sloppy smile, then looked around the room with his glass held high in a mock toast. "To Sabine Godard."

"Hear, hear," said a few of the others. Most just took the opportunity to sample their wine.

Crosshaven took another drink of his hock, but he kept his eyes on Lord Edward as he did. He'd noticed Lord Edward hadn't joined in the toast. "Don't be such a bloody bore, Ned," he said with a roll of his eyes. "You're not married yet, old man."

"True." But in three months time he would be. God, he was weary of this, of nights like this spent drinking or whoring and living as if there weren't something more to be had from life. He wasn't married yet, but wished Rosaline was already his wife.

Lord Edward put down his glass and stood. He felt a giant. With reason. He towered over everyone in the room, standing or not. "Good evening, gentlemen, my lords."

"What?" said Cross. He was a bit unsteady on his feet. "Are you leaving already, Ned? It's early yet."

Lord Edward could not bring himself to smile to soften his disapproval of his friend's behavior. Nor could he remain silent. "I do not care to hear any lady's character shredded for the sake of a man's reputation."

Cross focused on Lord Edward, registered the slight to his honor, and said, "She's no better than she ought to be."

"True," Lord Edward said. "But the consequences of indiscretion always fall hardest on the woman. Tonight, you are lauded for your seduction of the girl, deemed ever more manly. Your reputation as a cocksman is firmly established."

Crosshaven bowed amid a few catcalls. He straightened, grinning. Lord Edward was probably the only one in the room who wasn't grinning back.

"What reason had you to prove that fact at the cost of her reputation? No one disputes your appeal to the fairer sex." Lord Edward sighed. There was no point in lecturing Cross. No point at all "Tomorrow," he said with regret soft in his voice, "Miss Godard will not find the world so pleasant a. place. That is a fate you ought to have avoided for the girl."

"She's still no better than she ought to be, Ned." He pretended to sober up, but as a drunk would do. Sloppily. "I mean no disrespect, Lord Edward. But it's true about the girl. No better than she ought to be."

He acknowledged Cross with a nod, without smiling because he was disappointed in his friend. "Nor are you."

As he walked out, Lord Edward thought it was a very great pity that Miss Godard was so thoroughly ruined. Beyond repair. Crosshaven's boast of her would be everywhere by noon tomorrow. He did not know the girl person-ally but did not like to think of the disgrace that was soon to fall on her and her uncle. They would both be touched by Crosshaven's indiscretion.

He thought it likely the newly knighted Sir Henry Godard would put her onto the street.

CHAPTER 2

One year and eight months later, give or take a few days.
May 5, 1811

> *The former Lord Edward Murrack was now the Marquess of Foye and a guest at the palace of an English merchant in Buyukdere, Turkey, about twelve miles outside Constantinople. Europeans were not permitted to live in the city, and Buyukdere was a favorite summer residence for expatriates from any number of countries. Including England. A good deal of the diplomatic corps resided in Buyukdere, which overlooked the blue, blue waters of the Bosporus.*

THE FINEST WOMAN here tonight was Miss Sabine Godard.

How strange that he should cross paths with Miss Godard so many thousands of miles from home. Foye wasn't surprised to find she was a lovely woman.

If Crosshaven had noticed her, and, quite infamously, he had, it stood to reason she would have something. She did.

Foye sat on a chair not so far from the center of the assembly that he would be thought aloof, though he'd been accused of that and worse since he'd begun his tour of countries that had the single advantage of being far from England. He was not by nature a gregarious man and was even less so now, or so he'd been told by people who had known him before—True enough. For the second time in his life, he was a changed man. What a pity he didn't like the change

Now that he saw her before him, he understood why so many men had spoken of her looks and why Crosshaven had chosen her, it wasn't so much that she was beautiful. She wasn't quite that. A man didn't catch his breath at the sight of her. She was not a very tall woman, though from what he could see of her, her figure was a nice one. He stared at her, trying to pin down for himself the reason that she was a more attractive woman than she ought to be.

Her features were too strong for beauty in the classic sense, though anyone meeting her for the first time would think her pretty. She smiled often, and he'd watched several men stare, besotted, when her mouth curved a certain way. Her hair was an astonishing shade of gold. Curls at her temples and brow gave her an air of sweetness without being cloying, and there weren't many pretty young women who could manage that. A lace cap was on her head, a jade green ribbon threaded through the material. She wasn't beautiful, no, not that, but she was pretty. Exceptionally so.

She had something else as well, and he was determined to put a name to whatever elusive quality that was. What a shame Crosshaven had ruined everything for her. She might have done well for herself, had she stayed in London. There were any number of pretty young girls who'd married up. Some decent young man would likely have thought himself lucky to marry a woman like her. Foye couldn't help feeling at least partially responsible for the fact that she hadn't.

At the moment. Miss Godard was sitting at a table surrounded by men in uniform; sailors, soldiers of the Royal Artillery, Royal Engineers, or otherwise attached to the military here in Buyukdere. She was reading tea leaves for them and having a grand time, too. Despite her smiles, and despite the men gathered around her, she appeared unaware of the flirtatious looks and remarks sent her way, but not, he thought, unaware of her looks.

Miss Godard knew very well that men found her attractive, Foye decided. But she was not a flirt.

Her uncle, Sir Henry Godard, sat close enough to her that she could easily lean over and touch his arm should she care to. Sir Henry was deep in conversation with one of the merchants who worked for the Levant Company. The topic at hand, from what Foye could overhear, was the merits and demerits of St. Augustine. A heady subject for afternoon tea.

So far, Sir Henry had the advantage in the argument. He was a wily debater. Leading his prey to make admissions that seemed reasonable enough while, in reality, he was laying a trap such that when it sprang his victim would have no choice but to cede Sir Henry's entire point.

Experience had etched deep lines in Sir Henry's face and yet had taken a disproportionate physical toll on the rest of his body. His upper back was hunched, throwing his leonine head forward. His hair was that off shade of white, a yellowish silver, common to men who'd been blond throughout their adult lives. Notwithstanding the depredations of age and illness, Sir Henry was a man of considerable presence. His profession remained in his manner of speech, his temperament and even his gestures. It was easy to imagine him addressing a lecture hall of young men and terrifying them into listening at peril of their very survival.

The salon was filled with guests holding teacups and guarding plates of cakes, biscuits, and sugar wafers. There were tables piled with watermelon and bowls of sherbet in silver cups with delicate silver spoons. The merchant whose palace this was, Mr. Anthony Lucey, had invited only Englishmen and women this afternoon, though naturally men outnumbered the women, who were, for the most part wives or other relatives of the soldiers. Some of the men were employees of the Levant Company who had raised families here. A pretty English girl wasn't unheard of in Buyukdere. Not by any means.

Lucey himself, a longtime friend of Foye's late father, stood in the center of the room telling a story Foye had heard before about the time he'd gotten lost in Mayfair and had mistakenly knocked on the Duke of Portland's private door. Lucey was such an excellent raconteur the tale still amused more than forty years after it had happened.

He was beginning to think, though, that he ought to go get himself introduced to Miss Godard. Just to see what she was like. Naturally, he was curious. And since he was here, if the circumstances offered, he might explain what had happened.

Foye resisted the urge to smooth down his hair. There really was no dealing with his curls. They were contrary by innate disposition, it seemed. A good match for his face, which was one of the reasons he'd let his hair grow and never cut it short again. With a face that defined "ill made" and a body that tended to intimidate by sheer size—he had always been prone to muscle—Foye was used to women looking past him or away from him. Though since he'd become Foye, that happened marginally less often.

He plucked a crisp sugar wafer from his plate and took a bite. A touch of almond, he thought, and he had a taste of bliss melting over his tongue. Lucey's cook was superb, a Neapolitan man he'd succeeded in hiring away from the Italian ambassador's residence. The story of Lucey's raid on the Italian kitchen was amusing, too. Foye took another bite of his wafer and savored it while he watched yet another lovesick young officer beg to have his fortune told by Miss Godard.

Perhaps, he thought, it was something about the way she looked at a man. Yes. Something about her eyes. And her complete disinterest. What bold young man didn't want the very woman who wouldn't have him? Given all that he and Miss Godard had in common, he ought to at least meet her. It was, however, quite plain to him that to get anywhere with the niece one must start with the uncle.

When Foye was done eating, he asked Lucey for an introduction to Sir Henry.

The old man was formidable; that had been apparent even from a distance. Closer up, he seemed no less so for all that his frailness was the more evident. He had, Foye recalled, read one of Sir Henry's treatises, the 1805 *On Hubris.*

When Lucey walked him over to the philosopher, Foye was speared by a pair of iron gray eyes that would have been at home in a man forty years his junior, they were that bright and perceptive. He did not believe it was an accident that he should think back on his university days with some sense of dread. This man would have had no compunction whatever about sending a prince packing for want of preparation. No more a mere second son—all that Foye had been in those days.

Foye bowed when Lucey completed the introduction. Already the object of much curiosity on account of his appearance, more stares came his way when his titles were pronounced. Lucey, unfortunately, knew the entire list. Marquess of Foye. Earls of Eidenderry and DeMortmercy. He was used to them now, at last accustomed to the change in his identity from Lord Edward to Foye. There were days now when he could hardly recall a time when he hadn't been Foye. His first titled ancestor had been ennobled before the reign of Charlemagne. The Marracks of Cornwall had never been viscounts. Their nobility had begun with an earldom.

It was with him that the Marrack line would end. With the death of his brother without any living children, he was the last of the Marrack men. When he died, his properties and titles would revert to the crown. What a failure to take to his grave, to leave no one to carry on the name.

"Well, well, young man," Sir Henry said, laboriously craning his neck sideways to look at him. "That is a mouthful of names."

Foye smiled despite himself. He had not been called a young man for a good many years. It wasn't as though he was old, but at thirty-eight, he wasn't a boy anymore. Godard held out a gnarled hand for Foye to take, which he did, gently. The philosopher was crippled with the gout, and his skin was hot to the touch.

"Yes, Sir Henry, it is, indeed, a mouthful." He smiled, aware of Miss Godard's attention to their exchange. Would he tell her, if the opportunity arose? He ought to but didn't know if he would. She seemed to have made a life for herself here, far from England. Why bring up what could only be painful memories for her? Because, Foye thought, if he were her, he'd want to know the truth. "I hope you were not bored listening to all that."

"Not at all." Sir Henry bobbed his head. "I am pleased to make your acquaintance, my Lord Foye."

"The pleasure is mine, Sir Henry." Foye was aware that Miss Godard had stopped her inspection of someone's teacup—what nonsense that business was—to listen to the introduction.

Did she recognize his name from his connection with Crosshaven? Perhaps she did not know he and Cross had been friends and that Foye knew what had been done to her. Or perhaps she did, and now wondered if her reputation was to be ruined again by someone else who knew only the lies.

"Foye. Foye," Sir Henry said, tapping his chin with a finger permanently hooked into a claw. He narrowed his eyes and gave him a sideways look. "A King's College man, weren't you?"

Foye bowed. For a split second, he racked his brain for the essay he must have failed to write. "Yes, sir."

"Your elder brother, too, if I'm not mistaken."

"You are not."

"I thought so." Sir Henry grinned and nodded. "You were Lord Edward then, not Foye. That's why I didn't know who you were until you were close enough for me to see you." He pulled at a blanket spread over his lap. "Took a first in mathematics, didn't you?"

"I'm astonished you should know such a thing." It was at university that Foye had learned there were women who cared more for what he offered when they were intimate than for what he looked like in broad daylight. He'd also discovered he had a talent for pleasing his partners. He'd made himself an assiduous student of the delights to be had between a man and woman. Well.

No more of that for him. Those days were long gone. He was done with that life.

Godard waved a misshapen hand. "I made it a point to acquaint myself with the names of all the young men of promise. If we were at home, I would send Sabine to find my entry on you." He smiled, and the effect was disconcertingly sly. His niece looked in their direction at the mention of her name. "I kept a ledger, my lord. I followed you in Parliament, you know. Heard your maiden speech. I am rarely wrong in my predictions."

"Am I to be flattered by that?" Foye asked. He did not look at Miss Godard, though he burned to do so.

"I should think so. I saw you once or twice at university." He chuckled. "No mistaking you for anyone else."

He smiled again. "No, sir."

"I should think you learned early on it's better to have something here"—he tapped his temple—"than to have a handsome face. Too many young men these days spend hours primping at the mirror when they would profit more from improving their minds."

"Godard," his niece murmured. She put an arm on her uncle's sleeve in a gesture familiar enough to be habitual. Foye could easily imagine her needing to restrain her uncle's bluntness. For all Sir Henry's rudeness, he rather liked the man for it. He wasn't a pretty man, after all.

"What?" Sir Henry said, turning his torso toward his niece. "With a face like his, do you think he bothers much with enriching his tailor over his bookseller?"

"I think Lord Foye is very smartly dressed," she said.

"Thank you," Foye said. In point of fact, he was vain of his appearance. Even as Lord Edward, he had never walked out of his house without clothes that made other men beg him for the name of his tailor.

"Look at him." One thin arm shot into the air. "Do you think he spent his time at King's with his mistresses instead of in the library?"

Good God. Foye held back his shock at Sir Henry's speech. Miss Godard, too, felt the indiscretion, for her cheeks pinked up. Sir Henry didn't seem to think anything of his declaration.

"Godard." She slid a glance at Foye, and their eyes met. Hers were brown. There was nothing extraordinary about her eyes, but for the intelligence there. She was no ordinary girl, he thought. "Forgive him," she murmured.

"For what?" Foye said. "It's true. I am no model of masculine beauty. I am not offended by Sir Henry pointing that out." Age had its privileges, after all; and Sir Henry had to be nearer seventy than sixty. He had decided to be amused. There was brilliance yet in the old man.

"Sensible of you, my boy."

Foye nodded to Sir Henry, but he was absorbed by Miss Godard. She was a far more interesting woman than he'd expected. All this time, whenever he thought of Crosshaven and what he'd done that night, he'd been imagining a sweet young woman, weeping for her lost reputation. Naive and mourning the infamous wrong done her. Miss Godard was hardly naive.

"Have you been in Anatolia long, my lord?" Sir Henry said.

"No," Foye replied.

Miss Godard was now indisputably a part of their conversation. He could not help but look at her. Her eyes were not a common brown after all, but something a more poetic man might call dark honey. From the shape of her mouth, the tilt of her eyes with their thick, dark lashes, to the sweeping line of her throat to her shoulders, she was the sort of woman who made a man think of darkened rooms and whispered endearments. He understood very well why Crosshaven had chosen her.

"I arrived in Constantinople yesterday," Foye said to Sir Henry. "And you?"

Sir Henry folded his crippled hands on his lap. "We have been in Buyukdere coming onto a month. Is that correct, Sabine?"

She answered without hesitation. "In Anatolia, forty-three days. In Buyukdere, twenty-one, Uncle."

Again, Foye felt his understanding of Miss Godard to be maddeningly incomplete. Not a woman wronged and mourning her fate. Not a pretty girl who knew and used the power her looks gave her over a man. And to speak so crisply, with such unhesitating precision. He preferred it when the people he met fell into neat categories. Irascible old man. A young woman wronged. Foye did not yet know where to fit Miss Godard.

"Twenty-one days, my lord," Sir Henry told him with a smile that conveyed his pride in the precision of his niece's recollection.

The naval officer whose tea leaves she'd been reading bid Miss Godard adieu. She nodded, said good-bye, and though the officer waited for her to say something more, she didn't. For the moment, her table was empty of a companion, yet all the other men who had been waiting for their chance found themselves dismissed without a word.

"You have an able assistant, sir." There was an awkward silence during which Foye expected to be introduced and was not. He cleared his throat and returned a bit of the older man's directness. "May I meet your niece, Sir Henry?"

"What for?" Sir Henry's eyes scalded. Foye could only thank the Lord he'd never been in one of Sir Henry's lectures when he was at Oxford. He would have quailed under that gimlet eye. Because, in truth, he had spent more time with his various mistresses than with his studies.

"Godard," Miss Godard said, firmly this time.

Sir Henry tipped his head toward her. "Very well. I suppose there's no hope for it. Sabine, will you meet the Marquess of Foye?"

She stood to curtsey but did not extend a hand to him over the very small table at which she sat. He bowed in return. "Delighted to make your acquaintance, my lord."

"My niece, sir. Miss Sabine Godard."

"Miss Godard." He was aware he was staring too hard. She was still so very young. He doubted she was much beyond twenty. Crosshaven ought to rot in hell for what he'd done to the girl.

She cocked her head at him, and at that moment he would have given anything to know what she was thinking.

"Would you read my future?" he asked.

Sir Henry snorted. "It's nonsense, my lord," he said. "She knows that, too."

Miss Godard's gaze flicked to her uncle; she remained unruffled. "If he is on your list of men who will make something of themselves, Godard, I daresay he is well aware my tea reading is a nothing more than an amusing way to pass the time." She turned to him. "My lord, have you a cup you've been drinking? If not, you'll need fresh."

He pointed in the direction of the table on which he'd set his tea. "There."

"That should do." She smiled at him, but with no particular interest in him beyond what was polite and no indication that she cared anything for his title or his consequence. Or his lack of beauty, for that matter. How egalitarian of her. "I'll wait, my lord."

He returned with his nearly empty cup and sat on the chair opposite her. His legs were too long to fit underneath the table, leaving him no choice but to sit sideways or remain as he was with his thighs wide open. He turned on the chair. Miss Godard took his cup and looked into it. "Can you bear to drink another mouthful or two?"

He nodded. He would tell her, he decided. He would tell her about Crosshaven and then apologize for his role in her ruin, limited as it had been. He took back his cup, drank it nearly empty, and extended it to her.

"No," she said, refusing his cup. "Hold it just so and swirl the contents thus." She demonstrated the desired motion with her arm.

"Nonsense, all of it," Sir Henry said.

"Yes, Godard," she said without looking at her uncle. But he saw a smile lurking on her mouth. "Excellent. Now upend your cup on the saucer."

"Shall I first cross your palms with silver?" Foye asked.

"Certainly not." Her eyes, her very fine eyes, flashed with humor. There was more to Miss Godard than she meant to let on, he realized. "If I allowed you to pay me in order to learn your future, my ability to accurately assess what tomorrow and beyond may hold for you would be compromised."

"Consider the offer rescinded, miss."

Her mouth quirked. "Anyone who takes filthy lucre is no better than a rank charlatan."

Obediently, he swirled his cup and did as directed, upending the cup over the saucer. Though he did not like to admit it, she interested him. What was she? What had she become since Crosshaven? "And you, being above remuneration, are no charlatan, I presume?"

Her smile became a direct and knowing connection with his gaze. "I am the worst charlatan in Christendom if you believe a word I say, my lord." She righted his tea and stared into it. "This is utter nonsense, as you well know."

"My future?" He sighed. "I feared as much."

Miss Godard laughed softly. "Divination, my lord. As much as I admire the great civilizations of the past, I have concluded there is a reason men of modern learning do not maintain a belief in the ancient ways. Just as there were no gods on Mount Olympus, there is no magic by which one can infer the future from random patterns made in tea leaves." She quirked her eyebrows at him. "Or the entrails of a goat, for that matter."

He very nearly laughed. Nearly. My God, she was quick witted and not afraid to show him. "Nevertheless, this"—he indicated the teacup—"is, as you say, quite a charming pastime for a lady to have."

"Thank you." She raised her voice. "You see, Godard, that I am vindicated by Lord Foye."

"What's that?" Sir Henry said.

"The marquess finds the reading of tea leaves to be an amusing occupation." She spoke so drolly and with such affection for her uncle that Foye was hard-pressed not to grin. Miss Godard handled her irascible uncle quite well.

"More the fool he," Sir Henry said.

Miss Godard lifted a hand and pressed the other to her upper bosom. "A moment of silence while I read the portents, my lord."

She could have been an actress; the gesture and tone of voice were so perfectly done. No wonder the officers vied for her attention. For one thing, she was miserly with it, and when she did look at you directly, there was so much there to see in her eyes, a man could not be faulted for wanting more. He leaned his side against his chair, his elbow over the back, and stretched out one leg while he watched her. "I believe," he said in a low voice, "that we have a mutual acquaintance."

Without taking her eyes from his cup, she replied in a soft voice, "Not a mutual friend, I am afraid. Unless you mean someone besides the Earl of Crosshaven."

"I do not."

Her expression closed off. "You have a bouquet of flowers, here." She pointed to a mass of leaves. "That signifies you are to be happy in love."

"I was," he said. "Once. But no longer."

She looked at him. "I am not reading your past, my lord, but your future."

"Happy in love?" he said, looking into her eyes. "I fear that is quite impossible."

"The tea leaves never lie," she replied.

He wriggled his fingers over his cup. "Pray continue."

Manufactured by Amazon.ca
Bolton, ON

25134227R00072